MESQUITE JOHNNY

BARRY CORD

SAGEBRUSH
Large Print Westerns

First published in the United States by Arcadia House
First published in Great Britain by Foulsham

First Isis Edition
published 2017
by arrangement with
Golden West Literary Agency

A catalogue record for this book is available
from the British Library.

ISBN 978–1–78541–389–6 (pb)

Published by
F. A. Thorpe (Publishing)
Anstey, Leicestershire

Set by Words & Graphics Ltd.
Anstey, Leicestershire
Printed and bound in Great Britain by
T. J. International Ltd., Padstow, Cornwall

This book is printed on acid-free paper

CHAPTER
ONE

Deputy Jose Sanchez was sprawled in half somnolent peace in the chair outside the law office when he saw the rider come into town. He shifted his huge bulk, cocked one eye against the morning glare, and suddenly bounced to his feet with amazing agility for a man of his slow-moving disposition. He slammed the law office door open, stuck his head inside and yelled at the sheriff nodding over paper work on his desk.

"The orphan's back!"

The sleep whisked out of the sheriff's pale gray eyes. He swiveled around and reached for his gunbelt on the peg by his desk. Sanchez was already scuttling down the walk. Sheriff Marasek walked to the door and called him back.

Sanchez shook his head. He ducked into an alley, and Stanley Marasek sighed. Fun was fun, he thought, but it had to stop somewhere. He touched his puffed right eye and it helped to bolster his anger.

Other inhabitants of Mesquite Junction, warned by Sanchez's yell, took immediate action. Charley Greene, owner of the Red Dog Saloon, kicked his non-paying customer out of the coolness of his place and planted himself in his doorway, shotgun across his arm. Duck

Babson, across the street, hurriedly closed his door and barred it. Jake, the barber, put an "Out To Dinner" sign in his window and retired to the coolness of an inner room.

This flurry of activity spread beyond these establishments, and the drowsy peacefulness of the cowtown was disturbed by the violent slamming of doors and the muttered imprecations of men sorely tried.

The cause of all this commotion was an innocent-looking young man sitting indolently in saddle of a long-legged sorrel mare and seemingly caught in the spell of his own music. He was mouthing a jew's-harp to the tune of the "Cowboy's Lament," and the mongrel bitch who had run out to meet him paced the sorrel, her off-key howling providing a discordant accompaniment to the ragged rendition.

This was Johnny Delaney, better known in Mesquite Junction and the Big Bow ranges as "the orphan." He was a well set up youngster, tawny-haired and blue-eyed. He had a pug nose and a square jaw that was graced with a scant growth of sandy beard always scrupulously shaved. A Smith & Wesson .44 lay innocently in a scuffed leather holster at his left hip. He was ambidextrous, but he favored his left hand when it came to shooting. The usual carbine lay snugged in a saddle scabbard under his right leg, but he carried something tied to his saddle horn not usually considered standard equipment by the ordinary puncher. It was a set of red leather, twelve ounce boxing gloves, and they dangled by his leg against the saddle skirt.

He reined in in the middle of the dusty street, suddenly aware of the belligerent stares that greeted him.

The sheriff came toward him, balancing a Colt in his hand. Marasek was a rawboned man with a face burned the color of red saddle leather against which his pale eyes and bleached brows stood out sharply. At this moment his right eye sported a ring of yellow and purple and the inside of his mouth was cut and still slightly swollen.

He planted himself in front of the sorrel mare, his jaw tilting pugnaciously. "We're through celebratin' yore birthday, orphan," he announced grimly. "Turn that mare around an' head back. Celebrate somewhere else. "Try Gunsight," he added hopefully. "They're only twelve miles from here."

The orphan looked hurt. "What did I do?"

"*Do?*" The sheriff shouted the word. "Look at me. You an' yore fool gloves! 'Just a coupla rounds,'" he mimicked the orphan. "'Take the kinks outa yuh!' Hah!" He waved his right arm in a sweeping gesture that included the entire visible section of town. "A tornado couldn't do worse damage than you celebratin' yore birthday!"

The orphan slipped lazily out of saddle. "It's the heat," he dismissed the complaints carelessly. "C'mon. I'll buy you a drink."

Marasek shook his head, "No."

3

"Just one drink," the orphan persisted. He had an easy smile that was hard to dismiss.

"All right," the sheriff gave in, scowling. "I'll drink with you. But no more of yesterday's tomfoolery, kid. Keep those gloves anchored to that saddle."

The orphan shrugged, his smile showing white even teeth. "A li'l exercise ain't never hurt any man."

"I'll take my exercise on a bench in front of the office!" Marasek snapped. "I ain't as young as I was, or as spry."

Johnny put his hand on the sheriff's sloping shoulder. "C'mon, Granpaw," he invited with mock sympathy. "A drink'll put back the pepper in yuh." He chuckled. "Mesquite Junction needed a little livenin' up —"

"It's been lively enough for me!" Marasek growled. "It was plumb peaceful until yore brother dumped you off at the Sleepy H. Neither the Sleepy H or Mesquite Junction's been the same since."

They were turning to the Red Dog's steps when Greene's voice stopped them. "No you don't!" the saloonman said stubbornly. "I ain't lettin' that bobcat in here, Marasek. Nor you either if yo're with him! I had enough of the orphan yesterday. Tate's still nursin' his jaw in the back room, leavin' me to do all the work." The work consisted, during the somnolent daytime, of dozing behind the bar, but Greene's wrath easily magnified it.

"Tate needed the exercise," the orphan said innocently. "He was gettin' soft under his belt —"

4

"You busted two chairs an' a table an' laid Tate up so he won't be of any use for a week! Call that exercise?" Greene demanded wrathfully.

"No sense of humor," the orphan said, shaking his head. "C'mon, Marasek — we'll get our drinks at Nick's."

But the sheriff suddenly balked. "Some other time, orphan," he growled. He looked back to his office, remembering paper work that needed tending to. "But take it easy, kid! I let you run hog wild yesterday 'cause you were celebratin' yore birthday. But the fun's over. Any more ruckus an' I'll slap yuh in the calaboose till you cool off."

The orphan spread his hands in an innocent gesture. "You got me wrong, Sheriff. I'm a peaceful man."

Marasek snorted. The orphan grinned and turned away, heading down the street for Nick's. Greene relaxed and let his shotgun slide down gently, butt first, to the still. "Peaceful hell!" he growled. "Blastin' powder looks peaceful too, until somebuddy touches a match to it!"

Marasek was suddenly thoughtful. "Wonder what'll he do when he finds out Ferin didn't get back from Ladrone? Ferin was his sidekick, wasn't he?"

"He licked Lew Ferin twice," Greene conceded, "an' the poor fool cottoned to the orphan. Used to work out with Johnny in Nick's back room, whenever they met in town. Ferin was the only man willin' to mix it with the kid after takin' his first beatin'."

The sheriff scowled thoughtfully after Johnny's diminishing figure. "I hope he's smart enough to stay where he belongs. If he ever takes it into his head to ride down to Ladrone to look for Ferin —"

Marasek finished with a wry gesture, and Greene added almost unconsciously: "T N T on the loose!" Then he shrugged. "Aw, well, Stanley — he won't leave the Sleepy H. Not after what his brother told him. An' Andy's got enough troubles, I hear. Been losin' more beef than he cares to admit —"

"He an' Rawline have been after my scalp!" Marasek admitted. "But what the devil! Sanchez is a good man in town, but he ain't worth a hoot in saddle. An' I can't cover the Big Bow all the way to the desert myself."

Greene nodded in sympathy. "The rustlers must have a way of gettin' Sleepy H an' Rocking R beef across the desert. Rawline's outfit is closer. If he'd put more men ridin' line —"

Marasek spread his hands in a grim gesture. "The desert's out of my jurisdiction. An' if Rawline an' thet wooden-faced segundo of his don't like what I'm doin', they can —" He let his words dribble into the hot stillness, his gaze swinging back to the orphan, just turning into Nick's. "Just the same, if that bobcat gets it into his head to ride down to Ladrone —"

He shook his head slowly, not relishing the thought, nor the trouble brewing.

CHAPTER
TWO

The orphan swung jauntily down the street, ignoring the scowls that followed his passage. He brought the jew's-harp to his mouth and closed his eyes while he labored to bring forth the doleful strains of "Clementine."

He had been here five years now, but he remembered the first day he had stepped down from the stage in Mesquite Junction as though it had happened yesterday. He was a thin, edgy kid of sixteen, and he had come with his brother, Mike Delaney, to stay with Andy Harrison, owner of the Sleepy H.

Johnny had been his brother's charge since their folks had died of typhus way back when he was four. Mike had been father, mother and big brother to him, punching his way to rent and meal money under the ring title of "Tiger" Delaney. A welterweight, he would have been a sensation had he been thirty pounds heavier. But he wasn't, and too many years training in smoky back rooms, fighting in mining camp and city smokers, eating skimpily and living fast, had taken their toll. Mike must have known he was going to die when he dropped Johnny off at the Lazy H. Andy Harrison was their uncle by marriage, and Mike left Johnny in his care.

He left Johnny his worn gloves, a pair of faded purple trunks, and some earnest advice. He never came back. They got a card six months later. "Tiger" Delaney had died in a hospital bed — of tuberculosis.

It took a while for Johnny to get over the fact that Mike was never coming back. But his irrepressible nature finally found outlet, and in the next four years Johnny became known as "the orphan," which designation came to be synonymous with "local bad boy."

They called him wild and let it go at that, realizing that a youngster has to work the devil out of his system before he settles down. The orphan wasn't really bad, just full of the old Nick, his friends said. His enemies said other things.

Johnny wasn't expecting trouble when he headed for Nick's. The saloon was located at the extreme southern end of the dusty main street. A tired and skimpy oak spread crooked branches toward the establishment, and Johnny pulled up here and tied his mount in the scant shade. Turning up the steps, he cheerfully kicked the slatted doors aside and stepped inside.

There was no one at the bar, or behind it. He bellowed: "Nick!"

A long-necked man with crossed eyes stuck his bald head out of a rear room and swore mildly. "Might have known it'd be you, orphan. What do you want?"

"Yore company," Johnny grinned, stepped up to the bar. "An' a shot of that Taos lightnin' yuh got hid under the counter."

8

"Yo're too young to drink," Nick said crossly. "An' yo're makin' too much noise. I got a sick man back here."

"That so? Someone I know?"

Nick shrugged. "Rockin' R rider. Red Tanguey."

Johnny sobered. "Didn't he an' Lew Ferin ride down to look up an old friend in Ladrone?"

Nick walked to the bar. "Mebbeso. An' it looks like Red and Lew ran into more trouble than they could handle down in that border town. I found Red on my doorstep when I opened this mornin'. A slug in his chest. He musta ridden back across that desert, an' he was dyin' of thirst. Wrapped his reins around his left arm — an' his bay was with him, here, when I found him. I drug him into my back room an' went for the doc." He shrugged. "The doc don't think Red'll last the day."

"What about Lew?"

"Lew wasn't with him," Nick said. "Marasek was in here this mornin', askin' questions. Far as we made out, Lew disappeared in Ladrone."

Johnny pushed past Nick and headed for the back room. "I want to talk to Red," he said.

Nick followed him. "There's nothin' you can do, Johnny. It's the Rockin' R's business," he said seriously. "I sent a man out to tell Rawline. You better keep out of it, kid."

Johnny ignored the barman. He had come to like carrot-topped Ferin. The Rocking R puncher had a sense of humor that matched Johnny's, and though he was several years older, he and the orphan had taken to each other. If something had happened to Ferin, Johnny wanted to know what.

The back room was bare, except for a cot, a small card table, two chairs, a spittoon and a bad print of John L. Sullivan in characteristic pose on the wall. A dirty, unshaven man lay on the cot, partially covered with a Navajo blanket.

Johnny hunkered down beside the man. "Red," he said softly.

The man's eyes were open, but he was staring at the wall. Johnny called him again. Finally the man turned his head and his gaze met Johnny's. There was a film over the once bright blue eyes, and pain had made its run down his gaunt face.

"What happened in Ladrone, Red?" Johnny asked. "What happened to Lew?"

Red licked his dry lips. "Lew disappeared. Rode out with gambler . . . Tennyson. Left word he'd be back . . . later. Never showed up."

Johnny frowned. "Who shot you, Red?"

Red coughed. It was a weak, wracking cough. It took several minutes for him to get his breath back. "Was talkin' to Irene. In square. She —" He shook his head. "Rawline's job," he said weakly. "Man's job down there, kid. Keep out — of Ladrone!"

Johnny shrugged. "Lew was a friend of mine," he muttered.

Nick put a finger to his lips and shook his head. Red was coughing again. He turned his face to the wall, his shoulders quivering. Johnny got up and Nick bent over

Red, trying to ease the dying man. Outside, riders were pulling to a stop.

Nick motioned to the door, and Johnny left. Nick followed the orphan to the bar and set out drinks. "I called Marasek in soon as I got Red comfortable," he volunteered. "But Ladrone's out of the sheriff's jurisdiction. His hands are tied. That's why I sent a man to get Rawline. Red worked for the Rockin' R —"

Johnny nodded grimly, cutting in. "Lew was my friend, Nick. If he ran into trouble in Ladrone, someone ought to —"

"Do what?" a rasping voice demanded harshly.

Johnny turned on his elbow to watch Macey Rawline and his segundo, Joe Arlen, come into the saloon. Johnny held no love for either of these two men. Rawline was a hard-fisted bachelor with a reputation for dogmatic assertion and stinginess, and his foreman, Arlen, was a sour man of forty with no sense of humor whatsoever.

"Mind my own business!" Johnny snapped.

"A good idea," Arlen sneered. He walked to the bar, a lean, bony pole of a man with a hair-trigger temper. "Keep tendin' to it, kid, an' you won't get hurt."

Johnny's eyes went a slate gray. Nick hurriedly put in his say.

"Red's in the back room, Macey. I sent Tony out to the ranch soon as I got hold of him."

Macey nodded. He had a possessive attitude concerning his riders. "What happened?"

Nick told him what he had told Johnny. "Red didn't make much sense," he admitted. "Said Lew rode out of town with a gambler named Tennyson. He got plugged as he was gettin' ready to leave Ladrone. Right after talkin' to a girl named Irene."

Arlen's voice was sharp. "That all he said, Nick?"

Nick nodded. "Looks like he an' Lew got mixed up in somethin' down in that border sink hole —"

Johnny swung away from the bar. "Whatever it was," he said coldly, "I'm ridin' down there to find out."

Macey wheeled on the orphan. "Stay out of this, kid!" he ordered harshly. "Red an' Lew rode for the Rockin' R, not the Sleepy H!"

"I don't give a hoot in hell for the Rockin' R," Johnny answered bleakly. "But Lew was a friend of mine, even if he worked for you."

Arlen stepped between them, his long face unsmiling. "You heard the boss. Stay out of this! Ladrone's a tough town. Too tough for a fool kid to stick his nose into!"

Johnny stiffened at the plain insult, a sneer spoiling his good looks.

Arlen caught it, and an inner maliciousness made him add: "Ride on home, kid, an' grow yoreself a beard!"

Johnny nodded, the sneer widening to a twisted grin on his pugnacious face. "Sure, Joe. But first —"

Arlen said viciously: "Keep clear, kid —" and then he shoved his left hand out to push Johnny away while he dropped his right hand to his Colt.

Johnny slid under Joe's arm and hit him in the stomach. He hit the Rocking R segundo twice with his left hand and crossed his right into Arlen's face. The

12

Rocking R foreman bent over, as if bowing, then turned halfway around and fell on his face.

Rawline had turned around and was reaching for his Colt when Johnny tagged him. His gun cleared leather and flew out of his hand as Johnny smashed him with a vicious right. Then the orphan hit Macey again, two times faster than Nick could see.

Macey slammed into the bar and slid down into a sitting position against the base. He stared at Johnny through glassy eyes.

The orphan turned and stepped over Arlen's unconscious form to pick up his hat. He dusted it off and set it on his head at a cocky angle.

Nick was watching him, his mouth gaping.

"Send Tony out to the Sleepy H, Nick," the orphan said. "Tell him to tell my uncle I'm takin' a vacation. As of right now. I'll be back in a week to earn my wages."

Nick closed his mouth and threw up his hands. "Tell him yoreself!" he said angrily. "I ain't yore errand boy. An' another thing — some day yo're gonna —"

But Johnny was already out of the door. Nick followed him to the stoop and watched Johnny swing into saddle of the restive mare. Down the street, Sheriff Marasek had come out of his office and was walking rapidly toward them.

The orphan wheeled the sorrel and sent it at a run past the sheriff. Marasek waved for him to stop, but Johnny ignored him. The lawman yelled wrathfully: "Where you goin' now?"

The answer came back in a cloud of dust, cold and grimly humorous: "To grow myself a beard!"

CHAPTER
THREE

Nick was shaking his head as Marasek came up. The lawman's face was an angry red. "Damn fool kid!" he snapped. "Some day he's gonna meet up with some wrong gents —"

Nick jerked a thumb inside his place. "He just ran into Rawline an' Joe Arlen. Warn't altogether his fault, what happened, Sheriff. Arlen sort of goaded the orphan into it."

Marasek pushed past Nick.

Macey Rawline was on his feet, leaning heavily against the bar. Arlen was still out cold.

The sheriff stopped short and made a silent appeal to the gods with his hands. Macey shook his head as if to clear it.

"Where is he?" he asked Nick, coming in behind the sheriff.

Nick shook his head. "Gone to Ladrone, I reckon."

Macey swung on the sheriff, his face livid, the bruise on his jaw showing up vividly. "I've taken enough from that button, Stanley!" he bellowed. "I've got enough troubles, without having to take this from a younker. From now on either you put a bridle on him, or I blow him apart. An' if you don't like it —"

"Hold on!" Marasek snapped. He watched Joe Arlen turn over on his back and groan, and he felt somewhat relieved. "I don't know what happened here. But both of you are grown men. If you can't handle him, leave the kid alone!"

"We'll leave him alone!" Macey howled. "Next time he comes anywhere within fifty feet of me I'm goin' for my Colt."

Nick said innocently: "Better make sure he doesn't see yuh, Macey."

The Rocking R owner swung on the saloon owner. "That's the trouble, right here. The kid's an orphan — so everyone around lets him rampage like a spoiled yearling. What he needs is a good stroppin' on his back side — and if Andy Harrison wasn't a lazy fathead he would have done it a long time ago!"

Marasek scowled. "Mebbe yo're right on that, Macey!" he admitted. "But if the fool's gone down to Ladrone, he's either goin' to grow up fast, or we've seen the last of the orphan."

Rawline snarled: "There'll be no cryin' up at my place. I'm only sorry the fool's gone down there now. Mebbe you didn't know it, Stanley — but I sent Red and Lew down to Ladrone to look things over. Some awful smart rustlers have been drainin' my west range. An' there's only one way they could drive my beef — across the desert!"

Marasek nodded. "Harrison was in here last week with the same complaint. I told him to double his line riders, but he claims the thieves seem to know his moves."

15

Nick had crossed to the rear room. He was in only a moment; then he stepped out, his face serious. "Reckon you've wasted a li'l too much time, Rawline," he said quietly. "Red's dead."

Part of Ladrone lay across a disputed section of the Mexican-Texas border, which made it easy for the bunch of thieves infesting it to beat the law of both countries. It was a tough town far from the ordinary centers of trade, yet it channeled a surprising amount of business, both legal and otherwise, through South Pass.

Cut off from the more settled communities further north and east by a stretch of desert known facetiously by the hardy gentry who made the crossing as "Noah's Paradise," Ladrone was rarely visited except by men whose business there was urgent.

The orphan hit the desert about sundown and decided that with a rest the sorrel could make the trip across before daylight. He camped at a small spring and ate a can of beans which he kept in his saddle bag for emergencies. It was hardly satisfying, but it eased the ache in his stomach, and by morning he fully expected to be in Ladrone eating a hearty breakfast.

He checked the sorrel's picket rope to make sure the mare had access to the scant graze around the spring before settling back, and rolled himself a smoke.

The ride had allowed time for his anger to cool, and now, on the edge of the desert, he had a momentary impulse to turn back. Just what was he headed for?

16

Lew Ferin was his friend. But maybe Lew had gone off with a gambler named Tennyson on business of his own. What would he, Johnny Delaney, do when he got to Ladrone?

The idea didn't have the impact it had had back in Mesquite Junction.

He was a fool kid, wild, full of the devil. That's what they knew him as, back on his uncle's spread. A wild younker, handy with his fists. But not a man to be trusted with a man's responsibility. He rode for the Sleepy H because he was Andy Harrison's nephew — but he was never given a man's job. He was "the orphan" — the back East kid dumped on his uncle's lap.

He got up and threw his cigaret into the dark and stared into the night, thinking of his brother, Mike, and feeling suddenly alone.

He couldn't turn back now. He'd had his say, and now he had to back it up. If Lew Ferin was still in Ladrone, he'd find him. If he wasn't, then he'd find out where Lew had gone.

And maybe, in the process, he'd prove to Joe Arlen and the rest of Big Bow that he had grown a beard!

The sorrel looked rested when he saddled again, kicked the small campfire out, and mounted. He rode with a sickle moon over his left shoulder and the evening star a bright lamp ahead. His brother's training gloves rubbed against his right knee, and in the lonely silence they brought back memories of the man who had used them.

He had been riding for perhaps two hours, keeping southwesterly by north star, when he saw the wagon. It was a still night, and he could hear the creak and rumble of it before he saw it distinctly against the pale and desolate land. He watched it come on, heading at an angle across his path. Some freighter, he thought, taking advantage of the night to cross the desert.

He turned the sorrel and rode for the wagon.

The driver jerked the team to a halt and his whiskered companion reached between his legs for his rifle as the orphan came up on them. Johnny's Smith & Wesson forestalled the man's move and he straightened, his hands lifting clear of the Winchester.

The orphan reined in less than a yard away. "I ain't dangerous," he announced coldly. "But I don't aim to be misunderstood."

The driver hunched back in his seat. He was a squat, slovenly individual, and now his unshaved jaws began to work again on his chaw of tobacco. His whiskered companion, a long pole of a man with cold, watchful eyes, said mildly: "You hadn't oughta ride up on us like that, stranger. It ain't healthy."

From the interior of the covered wagon came a sudden medley of sound, as of a dozen shrill voices cackling in alarm. The driver turned and slapped his palm against the canvas, and the sounds cut off with frightened suddenness.

Johnny frowned. "What you freightin'? Chickens?"

The driver nodded. "Freightin' 'em into Barasol. We allus make the trip at night. Cooler."

Johnny nodded. "I'm headed for Ladrone."

The driver squinted at him before spurting a liquid stream of tobacco juice over the near wheel. "Ten miles — straight back," he said, jerking a thumb rearward. "You can't miss it."

The man beside the driver asked: "Puncher? Lawman?"

"Neither," Johnny replied. "Just driftin' through to the border." He pulled the mare away from the wagon, and the driver waved to him. "Wish you luck, pilgrim."

Johnny watched the wagon rumble northward, and when it dipped into a shallow wash he turned the sorrel and headed south. He didn't know that the whiskered man with the rifle had dropped off the seat as soon as the wagon hit the wash, nor did he look back to see the man climb swiftly up a small mound, kneel, and sight carefully against the night. Johnny was silhouetted against the stars and made a fair target for a good rifleman.

The orphan didn't hear the shot. The bullet gouged a deep gash over his right ear, exploding the night into a series of blue and blinding white lights. He fell forward under the impact of the slug, clutched instinctively at the horn and then, as he lost consciousness, he slid off. His right heel got caught in the stirrup and he was dragged a few yards by a frightened horse before it slipped free. He lay in a limp huddle against the pale earth.

The mare ran ahead for another hundred yards, then stopped, its fear suddenly subsiding. It turned a questioning head to the man on the ground and then began walking back, a sharp whinny questioning the night.

The rifle crack jerked the animal back on its haunches. It pawed the ground in a desperate attempt to get up. The next shot killed it.

The slovenly driver, standing up on his seat and watching, grunted his sparse admiration. "Good shootin', Pete."

Pete grunted. "Reckon I oughta go back an' make sure of him, Bunker?"

"Naw. If he ain't dead he's bad hurt, jedgin' from the way he keeled over. An' afoot in this blasted hell, he won't last the day."

Pete hesitated. "Jest the same I'd like to make sure. No tellin' who he is —"

"I tell yuh we got to make Barasol before daylight!" Bunker snarled. "Want to risk gettin' stopped again with these —" He jerked a thumb to the wagon interior. A frightened quiet pervaded the canvas.

Pete shrugged. "Yo're the boss, Bunker."

The moon was an hour down in the west when daylight cracked the rim of the earth and sent its ghostly heralds of light across the desert. Down the crumbly slope of a low hill a man moved slowly, pausing to watch the approaching dawn.

The orphan was lost!

His feet hurt and his head throbbed savagely. He had to rest often to still the waves of black nausea that welled up from the pit of his stomach.

The gash had bled freely down the right side of his face, staining his chin until he had wadded his handkerchief and pressed it to the cut. After a while it had stopped bleeding.

He adjusted the strap of his canteen, feeling a faint satisfaction that it was full. He could last a day on that much water. His boxing gloves dangled over his shoulder. He knew they were a needless burden, yet he was reluctant to discard them. The canteen and the gloves were all that he had taken with him when he had left the side of the sorrel.

This was lesson number one, he thought bitterly — lesson one in a hard game. He had played the part of a young fool, turning his back to them. But he had to admit that the rifleman had been good. *A moving target in the dark . . .*

The orphan shook his head slowly, and his eyes had a colorless quality. He would remember those two, when they met again.

They hadn't been satisfied with his story he was a stranger drifting through to the border, which in itself meant something. And they were freighting something more important than chickens . . . something they were willing to kill for.

He stopped thinking of the puzzle and concentrated on trying to piece directions from the gray jumble ahead. If he had kept his head he would have waited until it was light enough to follow the wagon tracks back to Ladrone. But he had been in a half-daze and had set out blindly in the general direction in which he thought Ladrone lay. Low cloud banks massed on the horizon had fooled him — he had taken them for the Ladrones, and now it was too late.

A low hill off to his left caught his attention. If he could make it before the sun got too high he'd climb it and take a look around.

The hill turned out to be farther away than it had appeared. The orphan's booted feet began to burn as he walked, and after a while they lost all feeling. The sun came up, cracking against the horizon clouds, spilling blood against their underbelly. Then it climbed until it was a white circle of incandescence, turning the blue sky into molten lead.

The heat hit the orphan liked a mailed fist. The alkali flats reflected the glare into his slitted eyes and dust gritted against his teeth. He began to get light-headed, and he brought his wandering thoughts under control and forced himself to give up the intention of climbing the hill and to seek shade instead.

He stopped and took a long swallow from his canteen, letting the warm water remain in his mouth before allowing it to slide down. His gullet reacted spasmodically and he had the almost irresistible urge to drink more — to keep on drinking until the parchment in his mouth was soaked up.

He screwed the cap on and slung the canteen over his shoulder. A line of scraggly mesquite trees lined the lip of an arroyo at the foot of the hill, and he sprawled down in their scant shade, lying like a lazy hound dog out of the beat of the desert sun.

He lay there, feeling weak and spent and discouraged. He'd never make it, but he refused to admit the thought. After a while he sat up and put his slitted eyes against the glare. The desert ran off into a deceiving flatness, hiding innumerable dry washes and gullies and small rises that took their toll of any man foolish enough to try to cross it on foot.

Better hole up here, Johnny, he told himself grimly. Wait until the day's done, then try to make it at night.

He sat up, crossing his legs under him like a Turk, and rubbed the lean flatness of his stomach. He took another drink and was putting away the canteen when he saw the rider.

He rubbed his eyes, thinking it was a mirage. But the image persisted. The rider was coming toward him, walking his horse in a direction that would bring him close to the mesquite fringe. He was a slim man in a brush jacket, and a dusty gray Stetson shadowed his face. He was either in no hurry, or, like the orphan, he was lost!

In any event, Johnny decided, he was going to provide transportation. He drew his Smith & Wesson and crouched in the shade, taking no chances of frightening the man away before he got within close gun range.

The rider came on at a steady pace, and just when the orphan thought he would pass within ten feet of him the man turned away and began to parallel the mesquite fringe. Johnny felt his legs quiver. He couldn't let the man get away from him now. He lunged out of the shade into the burning sunlight, his voice cracking: "Hey, you! Turn around an' head this way!"

The rider jerked upright in saddle and turned his head. Johnny took several quick steps forward, then suddenly stopped, his legs spraddled wide, a surprised look wiping the belligerency from his face.

The rider was a girl!

CHAPTER
FOUR

She stood staring at him, her hot and dust-streaked face tight with apprehension. The Levis and the brush jacket had fooled him, but there was no mistaking her now. She looked small and a little helpless to be riding across this strip of burning desert alone, but there was a determined cut to her chin and her blue eyes had no meekness in them.

Johnny lowered his gun, then nudged his hat back from his forehead with the muzzle. His grin had the old crinkle to it.

"If yo're a mirage, ma'am," he observed dryly, "then you've got me plumb fooled. If yo're not, then I'd appreciate it if you would give me a lift to Ladrone."

The girl shook her head. "I'm headed north. To Mesquite Junction."

"You were," he corrected her bluntly.

She stiffened. A flush darkened her cheeks. "Ladrone's ten miles that way." She pointed. "Once you get around Saddle Hill you'll be out of the worst of it."

He shook his head. "The spirit's willin', ma'am — but the flesh's weak. I'll have to ride." He lowered his gun and looked at it, like a man in doubt as to his next move. "I'd hate to have to leave you afoot."

"Oh!" the girl gasped. "You mean you're afoot?"

"You catch on," Johnny said. He added: "I had a hoss when I started. But I ran into a couple of hombres freightin' chickens to Barasol." His short chuckle was mirthless. "Guess they didn't like my face. They shore tried their best to spoil it. It's not my face so much," he went on, "but I shore hated to lose my cayuse."

The girl hesitated. He could see she was weighing his obvious need against some fear in her. Finally she nodded. "I'll take you to Ladrone."

He said seriously: "I'll not forget it. I'll be back in a second." He returned to the mesquite and picked up his brother's gloves, slinging them over his shoulder. He kept his back stiff, his pride refusing to let this girl see how weak he was.

She slipped out of saddle as he approached. "Get up," she said quickly. "I'll ride behind you."

"Ma'am," he said slowly, fighting the pounding in his head that was thickening his tongue, "I ain't never let a lady help —"

"You will now," she cut in firmly. She took his arm. "Here, let me help you up."

He pulled away from her and his knees buckled. He grabbed the saddle horn to keep from falling. The buckskin minced away from his sudden weight and his boots dragged in the sand. He fought to clear his head, mentally cursing the weakness in his arms and legs.

He got his foot into the stirrup and her boost helped him up. He sagged over the horn and held onto it with both hands. He felt her get up behind him, and her voice was soft in his ear. "Just hang on, cowboy. We'll be in Ladrone before noon."

It was past noon when the buckskin rounded the sandstone bluffs flanking Pima Creek and pounded across the heavy plank bridge. Johnny heard the hollow pound of the horse's hoofs and roused himself to glance with pain-filled eyes into Ladrone's wide street.

They rode quickly past the first few shacks, and then the girl turned sharply down a narrow alleyway that separated two sagging structures and pulled up before a long adobe livery stable.

A short, baggy pants oldster with a ten-day growth of tobacco-stained beard was sitting on a bench in the scant shade of the livery door. He jerked a clay pipe out of his mouth as they rode up and came to his feet, his jaw dropping.

"Irene! I thought you'd be in Mesquite Junction by this time!"

The girl said quickly: "I found him out in the desert without a horse. Take care of him, O'Leary!"

O'Leary made a wry gesture with his hands as Johnny slid out of saddle. "You shouldn't have come back. They've been lookin' for you all morning. Stew Parks an' Potsy. If they've seen you ride back —"

"I couldn't leave him out there," the girl said stubbornly. "I had to come back."

O'Leary suddenly stepped back, shaking his head. Johnny, moving blindly for the shade of the stable, heard the horses clump down the alleyway, and the girl's sharp cry brought him around.

27

Two riders came into the yard, cutting in between the girl and the street. The nearer one was a bull of a man, heavy and deep through his chest. He reached over and caught the buckskin's reins, tearing them from the girl's grasp. The other slouched over the horn, keeping his glance on Johnny and O'Leary. He was a thin runt of a man with a long sad face dominated by a blond, droopy, handlebar mustache.

The powerful man said: "You shouldn't have tried to run off, Irene. You've made yore dad mad."

"I don't care about my father!" the girl cried angrily. "And keep your hands off my horse, Parks!"

The big man grinned. "Now, now, Irene," he said mildly. "That ain't no way for a lady —"

Johnny pushed past O'Leary. "Take yore hands off her, you big ape!"

Parks turned a surprised face toward him. "You say somethin', bud?"

"I said to take yore hands off her, you fat ape!" Johnny repeated levelly. He had trouble focussing his eyes on the man, and his head ached. But he owed this girl something, for he knew now that she had been running away from these men when he had forced her to turn back to Ladrone.

Parks leaned over and backhanded Johnny across the mouth. The swipe sent the orphan reeling backward, and O'Leary, coming to life, caught him by the arm. "Stay clear of him, kid. That's Parks yo're talkin' to —"

Johnny shoved O'Leary away and walked back to Stew, who had ignored him and was turning away.

Johnny lunged at the man's stirruped leg, caught it, and shoved upward.

Caught by surprise, Parks tilted sidewise and slid down under the belly of his bay horse. The frightened animal stepped away, nearly walking on the cursing man, and Johnny fell on top of Parks and began pounding him in the face.

The big man grunted in amazement. He flailed away with an arm like a wagon tongue, and one of the swipes caught Johnny on the side of the head and spilled him. Nausea tightened the orphan's stomach, and he felt suddenly sick and blind. He saw Parks get to his feet and lunge for him, and he stepped in to the man and threw a punch. He felt it land glancingly on Parks' cheek. Then a hamlike fist exploded under his left ear and he twisted halfway around before he fell.

Parks stood over the orphan's body, breathing harshly. The boxing gloves Johnny had dropped lay in the dust just beyond, and he stepped over the orphan to pick them up. O'Leary and the girl watched silently.

Parks grunted. He pulled one of the mitts on over his big right fist, and his knuckles bulged against the worn padding. "Mebbe I can use these, Potsy. Protect my knuckles, huh?"

Potsy shrugged. "Come on," he said impatiently. "Mandell'll be waitin'."

The girl glanced back at Johnny's crumpled figure before they turned out of sight on Main Street. The sun was hot on Johnny's bared head, and O'Leary was shaking his head.

CHAPTER
FIVE

O'Leary waited until they had gone; then he bent over the orphan, got a good grip under the armpits and dragged Johnny out of the blazing sun into the shelter of his living quarters, walled off from the stalls. He found the youngster rather heavy and he grunted with the exertion of lifting him to his bunk. He straightened Johnny out on the worn blanket, then stood looking down at him, wondering if this was the man he was expecting.

After a while he went back into the alley for the orphan's hat and came back inside.

The orphan was stirring. O'Leary took a bottle of whiskey from his dresser and forced some of the spirits between the puncher's lips. Johnny coughed and pawed the bottle away.

The cut on his head was bleeding again. O'Leary tied his polka-dotted bandanna around the gash and wet it down with whiskey. "That'll kill the germs," he growled. He took a long swallow from the bottle then and eyed the youngster unsympathetically. "Yo're lucky. Don't you know enough to stay away from a man twice yore size? An' with a head like that?"

The orphan's grin had little humor in it. He sat up on the cot and put a hand to his head; then his eyes met the older man's with level coldness. "You know the big jasper?"

O'Leary shrugged. "Can't help it. Stew's the kind of gent everyone knows. Got the fastest gunhand, the hardest punch, the strongest back and the biggest mouth in Ladrone."

Johnny sneered. His head throbbed and he felt sick at his stomach, but he tried to get off the bunk. His legs were rubbery. He said: "Guess I'll have to stay with you awhile, Pop. I'm as wobbly as a new-dropped calf."

O'Leary took another pull at the bottle and wiped his lips with the back of his hand. If this kid was the man he was waiting for, his staying here was dangerous. If he wasn't, it was still too dangerous, for it would arouse suspicion.

But he couldn't just turn this hurt youngster out . . .

He went to the doorway and looked out into the stable yard, using this pretext to think. He had expected an older man, and a harder man — not a youngster who didn't even shave. But he had to know.

He came back, reaching inside his vest pocket for a coin. He held it in his palm for Johnny to see. It was a Mexican coin, notched with a triangular file. He said bluntly: "I'll match you to see if you stay here, kid."

Johnny said thinly: "Fair enough." He reached inside his pocket and found a silver dollar. O'Leary shrugged. This wasn't his man. They flipped coins and the orphan lost, to O'Leary's relief.

"Guess that's it," he said. He didn't look at Johnny. He was running a risk keeping him here, but the youngster didn't know it and he couldn't tell him. He said: "Here's yore hat. There's a sawbones down the street — up over the Mex barbershop. Drunk or sober, he'll fix you up."

The orphan nodded. "I had somethin' beside my hat when the girl dropped me off here. A set of gloves —"

"Parks thought he might be able to use them," O'Leary answered shortly. He turned and went outside, and the orphan put his hands on the edge of the cot and tried to hold the room steady in his gaze. He was learning fast. He had come riding to Ladrone as on a lark, and Arlen's words came back to him now, with bitter mockery: "Ladrone's a tough town, kid — too tough for a fool kid —"

Johnny had found that out. From here on in he'd be keeping his guard up and his chin protected.

He stepped off the bunk and waited for the room to steady; then he set his hat on his crisp hair with a jaunty tilt. O'Leary turned to look at him, and he said: "I don't know a soul in Ladrone, Pop. Except a girl named Irene. An' a gambler named Tennyson. Knew them?"

O'Leary looked at him as though he were joking. Then he shook his head, his lips tight and hidden beneath his dirty beard. And Johnny thought: He's afraid. He won't talk!

He said: "I'm sorry I bothered yuh, Pop," with lightly disguised contempt. He walked past the silent man into the blazing sunlight, and the heat made him momentarily dizzy. He turned left at the alley mouth and walked down the sandy street until he hit a stretch of boardwalk and the wooden awning cast a relieving shade.

A prim-faced woman with a basket under her arm stepped out of his way as he lurched by, her nose in the air, and he grinned sourly. He found the barbershop and the steep, dark flight of steps leading to Doctor Jay Valenti's office.

The hallway was gloomy. There was no window to relieve either the heat or the dimness, but on the door someone had tacked a card with this inscription: "Doc Valenti," and some cynic had added in pencil below the name: "God have mercy on your soul!"

Johnny knocked on the door and waited, hearing nothing but a heavy snoring within. He knocked again, then put his hand on the knob and pushed the door open.

The room was suffocatingly hot and reeked of whiskey and stale tobacco. The orphan grimaced. He walked to the window and let the shade up, then tugged open the sash. Light fell across the small man sleeping in a leather chair, his feet propped up on a stool, his hands folded across his spotted waistcoat.

The meager furnishings consisted of a black leather table, a mahogany-stained bookcase with dusty medical volumes, a rolltop desk littered with old letters, journals, bills. "Vanity Fair," a novel by Thackeray, in red leather binding, lay on the floor by the man's left elbow. A bottle of good Scotch was empty and had rolled away from the chair side.

Johnny walked to the door and closed it with a bang. The doctor stirred, rolled his head toward the sound, and squinted his left eye. Apparently satisfied, he turned away and fell asleep again.

The orphan walked to him and shook him. The doctor groaned. He opened his left eye again, squinted at the grim-faced man standing over him and said matter of factly: "There's bandages and antiseptic in the wall cupboard. Over there, by the door. And some water in the pitcher. Bring them here."

The orphan eyed him rebelliously. Then the humor of the situation got the better of his anger and he did as directed. The doctor pushed himself up to a sitting position and reached inside his vest pocket for a small blue-paper wrapper. He opened the wrapper and poured out a thimbleful of white powder directly on his tongue, then reached down under the chair and came up with another bottle of Scotch. He took a long slug out of the bottle and said: "Ah!" and shuddered. After a moment he motioned to the sink in the corner where a white-enameled pan was stacked against the wall.

The orphan obeyed with thinning patience. The doctor squinted at him. He was a thin-faced, dark man with a gray mustache and a gray goatee that gave his face the aspect of an anemic Satan.

"I'll take a look at it now, son."

The orphan drew up a chair and the doctor unknotted the dirty neckerchief, his nose wrinkling at the whiskey odor permeating it. He daubed a pad in alcohol and wiped the encrusted blood away from the gash. He worked swiftly, with deft fingers, shaking his head and whistling as he worked.

"You should be in bed," he said sharply.

The orphan shrugged. "I was thinkin' of it," he lied. He winced as the antiseptic burned. When the doctor began winding clean bandages around the cut he asked: "Where can I locate a gambler named Tennyson?"

Doc Valenti straightened. "Ah, the *Signor* Tennyson. He was a recent customer."

"Sick?" the orphan persisted.

"Unfortunately, he is now dead," Valenti answered. "Of lead poisoning, son."

Johnny got to his feet and gingerly replaced his hat on his head. "How much?" he asked grimly.

"Two dollars."

Johnny found the money and gave it to the man. The doctor took it almost indifferently. "Have a drink, son. It goes with the fee."

The orphan turned. "I need it," he growled. He found a clean glass on a shelf above the pump handle and poured a stiff shot out of the bottle. The Scotch went down smoothly.

"Thanks," he said. He was almost at the door when the doctor said quietly, "Tennyson had a girl he saw a lot of — name's Sally Ryan. You'll find her working at the Toreador, in the Mexican quarter."

The orphan paused and shot a look at the man. The other smiled. Johnny nodded and walked out. It was best to start at the beginning, he thought — and the beginning, according to Red, began with Tennyson.

Tennyson was dead — but maybe this Sally Ryan would supply what he had come for.

What had happened to Lew Ferin?

CHAPTER
SIX

The sun hurt Johnny's eyes and instinctively, like a wounded animal, he sought out the nearest lodgings. The Come Again House was the only hostelry in this part of Ladrone. It was a double-decker adobe with a gallery porch running clear around it on the second floor, and its bulk imposed itself above the rest of the structures brooding around it. It had been built by a man named Jose Santana, when Ladrone had been known as *Piedras des Ladrones* — foot of the Ladrones. But the Anglos from the north, taking over this border town, had shortened the name to Ladrone, and the new owner, a dry-voiced Yankee from Vermont, had not liked the mellifluous sound of Casa de muy Grande Ladrone and had renamed the hotel the Come Again.

In the lobby a tall, cadaverous man sat behind the desk, chewing sleepily on a broom straw. He pushed the register to Johnny, eyed the orphan's bandaged head with slight interest, and reached behind him for a key on a peg. "Number ten's all that's left, boy," he said dryly. "Make up the bed yourself, and keep your room locked. We're not responsible for missing gear."

Johnny signed. "Thanks for the advice, Paw," he said thinly. He was too tired and wobbly to argue. He went up the stairs with his head pounding and found room number ten was at the end of a long, dusty hall. He unlocked the door, barely looked around. Sun made a blinding splash in the middle of the room. He pulled down the worn shade and turned to the bed. He took off his boots and lay down fully dressed. He was asleep in five minutes.

He turned over sometime later to notice that the room had darkened. It was still stiflingly hot, but he fell asleep again. Later, he thought he heard movement in the room, but his drugged senses refused to respond. No one disturbed him.

A bright morning sun was slanting under the shade when he finally awakened. He was on his back, his holstered gun digging uncomfortably in his side, staring up at a dirty and cobwebby ceiling. He turned over, and paper made an unexpected crinkling on his chest. He sat up, frowning. His long sleep had replenished his natural energy, and he felt hungry as a gaunt wolf. He looked down at his shirt and pulled loose the ragged sheet of paper tucked between his buttons. The note painstakingly printed in block letters was short and to the point:

We know who you are. Get out of Ladrone pronto, or the next time this will be between your ribs. Savvy?

This evidently referred to a long-bladed knife stuck in the wall just over his head. Johnny pulled it and hefted it. It was a bone-handled, ten-inch blade of the old buffalo skinner's type.

Johnny's smile was cold. He didn't know who they thought he was. But if they thought they could scare him this way, someone was going to be plumb disappointed. He touched the bandages and prodded lightly at a point over his gash. It pained to his touch, but otherwise he felt all right. The cut was no longer bleeding, though any sudden movement of his head brought a faint throbbing that receded slowly.

He got up, stretched, and went to the wobbly dresser to look at himself in the scratched mirror. The bandages gave him a slightly pious air, as though he wore a halo. He grinned and fingered the light blond stubble on his chin, and for the first time since he had put a razor to his face he decided not to shave.

He went down into the lobby, forgetting to lock his door, and the cadaverous desk clerk called him over.

"You checking out, son?" he asked, almost making it a matter-of-fact statement.

"Not today," Johnny said coolly. "Why?"

The other frowned. "I kind of expected you might. After —"

"After what?" Johnny asked grimly.

The tall man shrugged. "Thought you might not like the service, son."

Johnny grinned at the confusion in the clerk's eyes. "It could be improved," he nodded. He brought up the buffalo knife and held it out in his palm. "Termites," he said mildly as the man's eyes popped. "You better look into 'em. They brought this into my room last night."

39

He gave a quick flip of his wrist, and the blade thunked into the wall behind the clerk's ear.

He turned leisurely and left the man standing open-mouthed. Out on the walk he paused, hesitating between looking up Sally Ryan and eating. His stomach won out.

Across the street a Chinese restaurant named the Green Dragon beckoned as the nearest point to still the clamor in his stomach. An empty, weed-grown lot separated the eating place from a long, shed-like structure bearing the name: House of Prayer. In Ladrone, Johnny speculated idly, there was need for prayer.

He was about to step off the walk when a harshly authoritative voice snapped: "Jest a minnit, son!"

Johnny made a slow half-turn to face the tall, long-strided man coming toward him. He noticed first the two low-slung Colts riding snug against the man's sinewy thighs, before his gaze moved up to linger on the badge displayed prominently on a dirty calfskin vest.

Skid Meskill was the law in Ladrone — the only law within fifty miles. A border tough, he had been hired to keep some semblance of law and order in a town overflowing with the scum of both countries. The badge on his vest and the authority it carried had swelled his self-importance until he had come to accept the town as his own — he was the final arbiter of who came and who remained in Ladrone.

The townspeople who had hired him were not concerned with his extra-legal business, or his pretensions. As long as he kept order in their business establishments and held thievery and violence down to a minimum, his methods went unquestioned.

He bore the full weight of his authority as he came to a deliberate halt in front of Johnny, planting his feet wide on the spur-scarred planking. His amused glance measured Johnny in one careless sweep, passing lightly over the S & W reposing in Johnny's holster. Meskill had browbeaten more than one gun-handy tough — this beardless youngster aroused only a fatherly interest in him.

"Goin' some place, son?"

Johnny frowned at the patronizing tone. After the incident in the hotel, he was in no mood to be talked to. But this man had a star on his vest, and Johnny had a certain regard for the authority it was supposed to convey.

"Headin' across the street for some grub," he answered levelly. "That against the rules in this town?"

The marshal hooked a big thumb in one of his cartridge belts. "Might be," he nodded, "if you don't keep a civil tongue in yore head. I'm Skid Meskill — marshal of Ladrone."

"Name's Johnny Delaney — an' I'm hungry," the orphan answered coldly. "We'll powwow later —"

Meskill's temper fired. "We'll talk now — an' *you'll* lissen! Every man who comes to Ladrone has to check with me. I decide if you stay — or go! An' as of right now, I'm tellin' yuh — clear out of Ladrone!"

Johnny shook his head. "Ain't got a cayuse."

"How'd you get into town?" the marshal rasped.

"Rode."

For a slim moment the marshal teetered on the edge of violence. Then he caught himself. He could feel eyes watching him, waiting to see how he would handle this cool youngster. He had adopted a fatherly attitude to this boy, and he was going to see it through.

"There's a stage in here tomorrow," he said. "You'll be on it when it pulls out. I'll be there to see that you do."

Johnny's eyes glinted. "Don't wait too long, Marshal." He started to turn away, but Skid put a big hand on his shoulder and hauled him around. "That's an order, son!" he snapped. "Now go on an' get yore feed!"

Johnny jerked his shoulder free of Meskill's hand. His eyes had turned a slate gray. "Don't lay a hand on me again, Marshal!" he said bleakly. "I'll get out of Ladrone when I'm ready."

The good humor went out of Skid's face as someone snickered behind him. "Reckon I've been wastin' my time on yuh, kid," he growled. "A week in the calaboose will —"

He stopped, staring with open mouth at the gun that had made a magic appearance in Johnny's hand. The muzzle of the .44 was only five inches from his belt buckle, and despite himself he shrank back, his right hand falling away from his own gun butt.

"I'm plumb peaceful," Johnny informed him. "But I ain't spendin' no time in jail. Not for mindin' my own business. When I get pushed I get stubborn. I've been told before to clear out of Ladrone. I'm stayin'. An' now, if you don't mind, Marshal, I'll continue on my way . . ."

He turned on his heel, sliding his gun back into his holster. Meskill watched him go, the cool effrontery of this youngster leaving him speechless.

The Green Dragon had a shabby exterior. It looked like a long shed, hiding its flimsy meanness behind a false front on which yellow paint had cracked and curled under the pitiless sun. Someone had painted a Chinese dragon in green paint above the door, and this alone had endured, defying the border sun.

Johnny pushed open the door and stepped inside.

The change from the dusty, glaring street was startling. From the frontier dinginess of Ladrone he had stepped into an Oriental world of rustling silk, of cool dimness, of muted sounds. The draperied windows allowed just enough light to see by, once his eyes got accustomed to the change. He found himself standing at the head of a long room flanked by semi-enclosed booths in which candles cast a flickering, mysterious glow. A variety of odors, most of them strange, struck his nostrils and found little response in him.

To Johnny, used to the rough and ready frontier lunchrooms, this did not look like a place to eat, and after that first startled moment he turned, determined to test his stomach with food with which he was familiar.

"Yes-s-s." The sibilant voice was at his elbow, and Johnny turned, wondering at the stealth of this man he had not heard. He was a small, slight figure dressed in mandarin robe, his hands clasped in front of him, hidden in the yellow silken sleeves. He wore his queue down on his back, and it was the first Johnny had seen of one of this man's kind. Johnny had seen Chinamen before — one of them cooked for the Sleepy H — but this man had a quiet dignity that impressed Johnny.

"I am Sun Yat Sen," the man said, bowing slightly. "Welcome to the Green Dragon."

Johnny hesitated. The man noticed, but he gave no indication of it. "We serve steak and potatoes," he said gravely, "and apple pie."

Johnny grinned. "That's my dish. Make it a double order on that apple pie."

"Follow me, please," the other said.

The orphan followed him down between the booths. Candlelight gave him brief glimpses of faces along the way. He was sorry he had come here, but his pride refused to let him back out.

He was halfway down the long room when a sudden small gasp from the booth at his elbow swung him around. He turned to look into a girl's startled eyes. It was the girl he had met in the desert.

She was sitting on the far side of a tall, spare-framed man with a sharp, ascetic face that went with the black frock coat he was wearing. He was a man of some fifty odd years, his temples gray, his mouth lined by a harshness not touched by mercy.

44

Facing him across the table sat a younger man, quietly dressed in town clothes. He was a slender man, with a thin, scholarly-looking face enhanced by black sideburns that reached midway down his cheeks. He looked harmless, but Johnny's glance picked up the bulge of a shoulder holster under the broadcloth coat, and then his gaze, meeting the man's eyes, met a hostility so sharp and unexpected that it tensed him.

The girl was looking down at the table, not meeting his glance. But it was the girl he had forced to ride him back to Ladrone — even though she had discarded her mannish range garb for a plain brown taffeta dress that did not become her. This was Irene, the girl Red Tanguey had mentioned — the girl who had talked to Lew Ferin.

"Hello," he said boyishly, and then, remembering his hat, he removed it. His crisp tawny hair curled over the slightly soiled bandage around his head — but the candlelight was kind to him, softening the lines pain had scribbled under his eyes. "Hello — Irene."

The girl looked up at him. Across the table the younger man said sharply: "You know this boy, Sis?"

"I found him in the desert," the girl said tonelessly. "He was hurt. I brought him in to Ladrone."

The older man turned to Johnny, measuring him with a stern, disapproving eye. "Another sinner drawn to the wickedness of this evil town. Another soul headed for damnation." The words rolled easily from his harsh lips, while his eyes lighted as with a far away fire. "Young man!" he intoned, his voice almost sonorous in that still room, "leave this den of iniquity

45

before it is too late! Before the hardened sinners of Ladrone drag you too far down along the road from which there is no return —"

Irene placed a hand on the man's arm, stilling him. "Father, please!" Her eyes met Johnny's. "Mr. Delaney — my father, Clay Mandell. And my brother, Henry —"

"Iron Mandell!" the younger man corrected her coldly. And Johnny saw now that this man's arm terminated at his wrist and a curved, three-pronged claw replaced his left hand.

"It's been a long time since it was Henry, Sis — remember?" he reminded her. He turned his glance to the orphan, his dislike naked on the bright surface of his blue eyes. "You heading through to Mexico, kid?"

"Wasn't aimin' to," Johnny answered. He was conscious, suddenly, that Sun Yat Sen was waiting by an empty booth further down. But he had come to Ladrone to find Lew Ferin, and this girl had known Lew.

"My sister said she ran into you out in the desert, north of here," Iron Mandell persisted. "Running from trouble — or looking for it?"

"I usually meet it halfway," Johnny answered levelly. Then, deliberately ignoring the man, he addressed the girl, sitting stiff and strained by the wall. "I didn't have a chance to say thanks yesterday. I'd like to say it now —"

"Say it — and move on!" Iron Mandell bit out.

Johnny held back the sudden surge of his temper. After all, this man was her brother!

46

"I've come to Ladrone to find a friend of mine," Johnny said quietly. "Name's Lew Ferin. I heard you knew him —"

He saw the fear flare up in her eyes before she shook her head. "You must be mistaken, Mr. Delaney. I know of no such person."

"He came to Ladrone about two weeks ago," Johnny persisted. "Rode in with a lanky redhead named Tanguey. Both men rode for the Rockin' R, a big spread across the desert."

Irene Mandell avoided his eyes. "I'm sorry," she said in a voice that was almost a whisper. "I've never met anyone named Lew Ferin."

Iron Mandell came to his feet in the narrow space between table and booth wall. He twisted to face Johnny, and they were of a height. "You insolent young fool!" he rasped. "A lot of men drift through Ladrone on their way into Mexico. Are you insinuating that my sister —"

"Henry!" Irene's tone was sharp, cutting his statement short. Her face was still white, bloodless — but there was a sudden temper in her eyes that held her brother. "I'm sure Mr. Delaney had no such thoughts."

Johnny nodded slightly. "Thank you, Irene. I'm sorry if I've bothered you. If I can in any way repay you for —"

"You can get out of Ladrone!" Iron Mandell said tightly. He was wound up, primed for trouble, and neither his father's warning glance nor his sister's disapproval would stop him. "There's enough trouble here without strangers butting in where they don't belong!"

"Coming to Ladrone is my business," Johnny said pointedly. He didn't want trouble with this man, but he saw it coming and he knew he couldn't avoid it. And his temper, suddenly slipping its leash, poured the thin acid of contempt into his voice. "I've been minding mine, Mandell — you'd sound better sticking to yourn."

Mandell cursed as he swung. Johnny saw it coming and moved his head aside, a bare three inches. It was enough to cause Mandell to miss, to lose his balance in the narrow confines of that booth. He fell across the table, jarring it into his father's lap, spilling the wine bottle over the tablecloth. The candlestick skidded to a precarious balance on the table edge before Irene caught it.

Mandell's claw gouged its triple groove in the table top as he twisted to get to his feet. The tablecloth came up with him, jerking the bottle and glasses to the floor.

Clay Mandell lunged across the table, his big hands pinning his raging son against the booth wall. "Easy, son!" he said impatiently. "You're making a fool of yourself."

The words got through to Iron Mandell. He stood still while Clay pulled the tablecloth free and spread it over the surface of the table. His face was dark with a burning humiliation that was not nice to see.

Clay turned to Johnny. "My son was offering you sound advice," he rasped. "Ladrone is already overflowing with disreputable characters like you — men who swagger down the streets looking for trouble —"

48

"This is the third time in less than an hour I've been given that advice," Johnny interrupted dryly. "I was told to keep away from Ladrone before I came here. A *muy malo* town. So far I've run into a four-flushing town marshal, you — and, oh yes, a jasper named Stew Parks." Anger pushed a sneer across Johnny's face, spoiling his boyish good looks. "I don't like being pushed around — or lectured to. I owe something to your daughter — but I owe you nothing. You leave me alone an' I promise you I'll look after my soul, sinful as it may be."

He looked at Irene Mandell, his voice softening. "You were runnin' away when I made you come back to Ladrone. If you ever want to leave again — let me know. I'll see that you get to Mesquite Junction."

He turned on his heel.

Only then did Iron Mandell sit down, his whole body shivering with the intensity of his feeling.

"A rash young man," Clay Mandell murmured. "He won't be easy to get rid of."

Irene's voice was bitter. "Leave him alone. I'll tell him nothing. He'll leave Ladrone soon enough —"

Clay Mandell shook his head. "You brought him here, girl. And you heard what he's after. He's looking for Lew Ferin." Clay's eyes had a strange, thoughtful glitter. "You never told me you knew Ferin."

"I don't!" the girl said wearily. "He came to see me at the hotel. Said a gambler named Tennyson had sent him. He wanted to know how to get to Canyon Verde."

"Why?" Clay asked softly. "What did he want at Canyon Verde?"

Irene shook her head. "He didn't tell me."

"But you ran away, a few days later," her father pointed out. His voice was low, falsely gentle. "Why did you do it? What have we done to deserve it?"

The girl lifted her face, but her eyes remained focussed on the booth wall. "I'll run away again!" she said defiantly.

Her father sighed. "You were a year old when your mother died, Irene. I tried to take her place. If sometimes I've not been too gentle, you must remember this is a wicked world, daughter. My calling has its heartaches, its troubles. The world is full of sinners in need of salvation. I try to do my modest bit, but sometimes —"

"Save your sermon," Irene interrupted. "Long ago I found out you were a fake. A thief. You — and Henry. Posing as honest men." Her laughter was restrainedly bitter. "Sky pilot Clay Mandell. Border town savior!" She turned on him, her eyes blazing with a mixture of hurt and contempt. "I'm your daughter," she breathed intensely, "but I don't have to live your kind of life. I'll run away again. And next time you'll not find me —"

Clay's hand closed over her arm, hurting her. "You'll stay," he said harshly. "I'll kill you before I let you go."

Iron Mandell's claw made a rasping sound across the table. "Let go her arm!" he said. His voice was small, caught in his throat. Little beads of sweat lay like drops of water on his brow. His voice thickened. "*Let go her arm!*"

50

His father drew his big hand away. "You're a fool, son!" he breathed. "Some day you'll regret this!"

Iron Mandell ignored him. "I'm sorry you feel that way, Irene," he said. His voice was shaking, as if he couldn't control it.

"So am I, Henry," Irene murmured. She was the only one who still called him by his given name. Even her father called him Iron Mandell.

She looked into his face, trying to remember the boy she had grown up with. She had been with him the afternoon he had come home, his left hand mangled by a shotgun blast. She had been with him while the doctor amputated that hand above the wrist. Henry Mandell had been fourteen then, a slim dark youngster with a quick mind, a sensitive soul, a stormy temper.

Ten years ago.

The boy she had known had gotten lost in those years, and Iron Mandell had emerged. A hard and emotionally unstable man who had never adjusted to the loss of his hand.

And in the years since they had moved from Sonora — moved restlessly back and forth across the border — she had come to know her father for what he was.

All she wanted now was to get away from them. All her instincts rebelled at the duplicity of her life, the violence that always followed them. She wanted to be free of this. But the blood tie between them was a bondage — a bondage her father enforced.

"It was a foolish thing to do," Clay Mandell repeated coldly. "Running away like that. Don't ever try it again!"

Irene didn't answer.

CHAPTER
SEVEN

The Mandells had gone by the time Johnny finished his second helping of apple pie. He lingered over coffee, rolling himself a Bull Durham. He had gotten nowhere concerning the whereabouts of Lew Ferin. The gambler Tennyson was dead — and Irene Mandell had disclaimed knowing Lew.

Had she lied?

She had not been at ease when he had talked to her. She had been close-mouthed, strained. She had acted like a woman held captive, and Johnny remembered she had been running away when they had met.

Running from whom? Her father and brother?

Nor could he explain the belligerency of the Mandells toward him. The repeated warnings to get out of town he had received. The note pinned on his shirt in his hotel room. The marshal's order. Iron Mandell's insistence. The man's dark, intense face came back to Johnny, and the orphan frowned. Iron Mandell had acted like a jealous man. Jealous of whom? His sister? It didn't make sense.

Whatever Lew Ferin had gotten himself mixed up in, Johnny reflected grimly, it was no small matter. It could be that Tennyson had been killed because of it. And he,

Johnny Delaney, had so far merely been warned because they didn't take him seriously. Just a fool kid sticking his nose in where he didn't belong. A grin flickered across Johnny's lips. There were some surprises due in Ladrone.

He had one lead left, but he had a sudden hunch this one would pay off. Sally Ryan, the dancer at the Toreador.

After the cool dimness of the Green Dragon, the glare outside hurt his eyes. He paused on the walk, tilting his hat down over one eye. It gave him a sudden hard appearance, and he chuckled softly as he ran the knuckles of his hand across the blond stubble on his chin.

He asked directions of the first man he met. "The Toreador?" the man repeated. "Shore. Down in the Mexican quarter. First dive as you turn left down the *Avenida de Villa*." He turned to watch Johnny as the orphan headed down the street.

The Mexican quarter lay in Mexico, and thus, legally, was outside the jurisdiction of the men who ran Ladrone. Mescalero Creek, a dry gully that ran water only for short periods during the rainy season, bisected the town. In the days before Texas had broken away from Mexico, Ladrone had suffered no boundary troubles, being then entirely Mexican. Mescalero Creek had no particular significance until the birth of the Republic of Texas. Then it became the boundary line between two countries, and Ladrone, a homogeneous village, suddenly found itself bisected and, with the advent of hard-eyed newcomers from the north, also bilingual.

The Toreador, situated as it was just across the plank bridge spanning the creek, attracted to it the worst elements from both sides of the Line. Mexican *bandidos* rubbed elbows here with taller, hard-eyed men wanted by the law north of the Border. The liquor was raw and potent, and no one questioned the man at his elbow.

Johnny Delaney crossed the bridge under a broiling midday sun and found the Toreador almost deserted. A small, wizened Mexican was desultorily sweeping the floor. Two villainous-looking Mexicans with cartridge bandoliers slung across their chests, old model carbines at their feet, and huge anthill sombreros shading their dark faces, were arguing over a bottle of *pulque*.

Johnny paused just inside the doorway. No one even bothered to look at him. Evidently, the orphan reflected cynically, the Toreador's business was mostly among the night trade.

Chairs were stacked up along the adobe side walls. A small box piano, scarred by careless handling and many cigaret burns, stood close to a low wooden platform which was either used for dancing, or from which entertainers did their acts.

For a brief moment he wondered what a girl with a name like Sally Ryan would be doing in a dive like this.

The old swamper swept his way toward Johnny, his head down, lost in his senile thoughts. The orphan sidestepped him and headed for the bar where a huge, moon-faced man was snoring so loudly that the glasses on his shelf rattled.

Johnny put his right foot on the dented rail and stared curiously at the barman. The man must have weighed all of three hundred pounds. He was sitting on a stool, his broad back propped against the bar where the counter made an L hook and anchored against the rear wall. His dirty apron, covering a barrel stomach, heaved and collapsed to his breathing.

The orphan pounded on the bar top.

The barman stirred. One eyelid went up, and a beady black eye surveyed Johnny. The eye closed and the snoring resumed.

Johnny frowned. He reached over, prodded that mountainous bulk. "Yuh got a customer," he growled. "Wake up!"

The barman stirred. He put a huge, hairy forearm on the counter and heaved himself up. Standing, he loomed half a foot over Johnny.

Johnny tossed a half-dollar on the counter. "Tequila," he said coldly. "And some information, when you wake up."

The big man put a palm over the half-dollar and blinked his eyes. The two craggy customers behind Johnny had ceased their quarrelling and were grinning at the barman.

"*Si*, Tando!" one of them laughed. "Geeve the *muchacho* what he asks. Or he may cause *mucho* trouble, eh?"

Tando shook his head. He pushed the half-dollar toward Johnny. "Go home," he grunted. "I do not serve *muchachos* here. Only men weeth wheeskers."

The orphan's voice was level. "I said tequila, Fat Boy. Don't let my face fool you. I'm twenty-one."

"Geeve heem meelk, Tando!" the raspy voice sneered from behind Johnny. "Eet would be a pity to waste good tequila on heem."

Tando grinned. The sleep had gone from him, and as he looked at this smooth-faced youngster who had evidently wandered into his place by mistake, he saw a chance to liven the dull afternoon.

Reaching under the counter for the pail of goat's milk he kept as a favor for some of his customers with children, he poured out a glass. "Thees ees on the house," he grinned, sliding the glass to Johnny.

Johnny's voice was grim. "Yo're wrong!" he snapped. "This is on you!" He lifted the glass and flipped the milk into Tando's face.

For a long moment surprise held Tando motionless, milk dripping down his chin, making a small, plopping noise on the counter. Then he shook himself, like a bear rousing. With a growl he reached a hairy arm across the bar for Johnny's throat.

The orphan's right crossed under that arm and exploded flush on Tando's jaw. The big man rocked back against the shelves; then his knees suddenly buckled and he slid down out of sight.

Johnny swung around. The pair of craggy customers had come to their feet, scowling with surprise.

"You gents want a hand in this?" Johnny asked dryly.

The nearest hombre clamped his hand around the neck of the wine bottle and lunged for Johnny. The orphan jabbed the man's upraised arm before he could complete his swing, and the bottle jarred out of his hand and smashed against the bar. The Mexican's rush carried him in close, and Johnny doubled him with a left hook that sank wrist deep into the man's stomach. His right, following through, dumped the man limply across a spittoon.

Johnny had moved fast, and the swift pacification of the first man had caught the other flat-footed. He backed away now, the scowl tightening on his swarthy face. From somewhere on his person he palmed a knife, a long-bladed balanced weapon whose glitter matched the ugly glint in his eyes.

"Maybe you can dodge thees!" he hissed.

Johnny's left hand dropped to his gun. A wreath of smoke shrouded his hip and the heavy report smashed its answer across that room.

The swarthy man caught his bleeding hand in the palm of his other and pressed both to his stomach. The shock of that bullet as it had scarred his fingers, wrenching the knife from them, acted as a momentary anesthetic — the pain would come later.

He stared at Johnny, his eyes wild; then he turned and plunged out of the saloon, his boots making a rapid thudding that faded slowly.

In the heavy silence that returned, Tando's deep, awed voice was almost reverent: "*Por Dios!*" Then he began to laugh, a big, belly-rolling sound that boomed across the room.

Johnny swung around, the S & W in his fist. Tando had evidently shaken off the effects of Johnny's smash almost immediately. He was bent over the counter, a bottle in his huge hand, and evidently he had intended to use it.

"*Por Dios!*" he repeated, still laughing, and set the bottle down on the bar instead. "I theenk Antonio ees steel runnin', eh, *muchacho?*"

Johnny slid the S & W back into his holster. "Johnny Delaney's the name!" he growled. "An' what in blazes is so funny?"

Tando craned over the bar and looked down on the customer curled over a spittoon. He shook his head, his laughter bringing tears to his eyes. "Geeve heem meelk, they said!" he roared. "An' now Antonio is steel runnin', like the *diablo* heemself is behind heem. An' poor Jose —"

Johnny grinned. Despite himself he found himself warming to this huge man who could laugh when the tables were turned against him.

Tando wiped his eyes with a corner of his apron. Turning, he fetched two clean glasses. "May I have the pleasure, Señor Delaney?" he said gravely, pouring from a bottle. "The tequila ees on the house."

Johnny shrugged. He picked up his glass, nodded, and tossed the pale liquid down. His hand, coming down to place the glass on the bar, froze. A small, strangling sound rattled in his throat. His left hand clutched at the bar for support, and he coughed violently. The fire in his throat finally burned itself out and he wiped his eyes with the back of his hand. "Holy cow!" he said weakly. "So this is tequila?"

Tando had absorbed his without blinking. Years of close familiarity with the brand of pale dynamite had lined his throat and stomach with an insulation tequila couldn't penetrate.

"Eet weel put the hair on yore chest, Johnny," he encouraged the youth. "Let me —" he offered generously.

The orphan put his hand over the mouth of his glass. His eyes were still watering. "Mebbe I'd do better on goat's milk at that," he muttered.

Tando looked disappointed. "You asked for tequila," he reminded Johnny.

"Some other time," Johnny said. Jose was stirring, groaning weakly, and the orphan bent, got a grip under the man's arms, and dragged him across the room to a chair against the wall. He propped the dazed man carefully on his seat and walked back to the bar.

"This way I can talk to you an' keep an eye on him," he explained casually.

Tando nodded. "I do not have many customers from across the Mescalero at thees hour," he said shrewdly. "You here by meestake — or you are lookin' for someone. *Si?*"

"*Si,*" Johnny answered. "I came to see a Miss Ryan. Sally Ryan?"

Tando's lids half closed. "For why?" he asked softly.

"She works here, I understand?"

Tando nodded. "For why?" he repeated.

"This girl knew a gambler named Tennyson pretty well," Johnny said. "An' Tennyson was a friend of Lew Ferin's!"

Tando's voice had no inflection. "An' thees Lew Ferin —"

"Is a friend of mine," Johnny finished coldly. "He rode into Ladrone with a redheaded cowpoke from up north. About two weeks ago. The redhead came back across the desert, with a bullet in his lungs. Lew Ferin never showed up."

Tando poured himself another drink and tossed it down with the gesture of a man with other things on his mind. "An' you theenk Sally Ryan can help you?" he asked quietly.

Johnny shrugged. "She's my last lead," he admitted. "Tennyson is dead. An' Irene Mandell won't talk."

Tando licked his thick lips. "You know what you are gettin' into, Johnny?"

The orphan turned so that he faced Jose, who was sitting up, shaking his head. "I'm beginnin' to find out," he said coldly. "Since I've come to Ladrone I've received four warnings to clear town. But I'm a stubborn cuss, Tando. I don't like gents shovin' me around."

Jose came to his feet. He braced himself, muttering curses. Tando's voice cut gruffly across his Mexican tirade. "Vaya, Jose."

Jose hesitated, his anger riding the dark flush on his cheeks. Tando reached under his bar and brought up a sawed-off double-barreled shotgun. "Pronto!" he added softly.

Jose found his hat, clapped it on his head, and went out.

Johnny turned back to the huge barman. "I'm still askin'," he reminded the other quietly. "I'd like to talk to Sally Ryan."

Tando looked toward the rear of the saloon, his round face creasing in a thoughtful frown. "They keeled Tennyson," he muttered, as if reminding himself. "He was one of them, Johnny — but they keeled heem. Because he knew thees friend of yours — thees Ferin. That much I know."

Johnny's face was grim. "Ferin? Did they kill him, too?"

Tando shrugged. "I don't know."

"Does Sally Ryan?"

Tando shook his head. "But I weel tell her, Johnny. At sundown, she weel meet you. South of Ladrone, past the canyon bend where Ladrone Creek turns west, there ees a tree — a Joshua tree. Ride there and wait. Sally weel meet you. When the sun has gone down, Johnny."

"How do I know she'll be there?" Johnny questioned.

"By all the saints, I promise," Tando growled. "She'll be there."

Johnny was suspicious. "Why?"

"Because," Tando said slowly, "Sally Ryan ees my sister!" He saw Johnny's lips twist unbelievingly, and he added harshly: "She married thees gambler, Tennyson, three years ago. Hees name was Paddy Ryan. But always he was known only as Tennyson." Tando poured himself another drink. "He was one of them, Johnny — but he was good to my sister. An' they keeled heem!"

He tossed the drink down, his eyes suddenly black and ugly. "Now you believe me when I say my sister weel be there? *Si?*"

Johnny nodded. "Thanks, Tando." He put out his right hand. "Sorry for that crack on the jaw."

Tando fingered the bruise on his chin and suddenly grinned as he took Johnny's hand in his huge paw. He looked down at the comparatively small fist in his, and he began to shake his head in wonder.

Johnny withdrew his hand and rubbed his bruised knuckles. "You've got a hard jaw, Tando," he grinned. "But an easy target. Next time, keep it covered." He turned on his heel, thumbing his hat on his head, and he was whistling as he went out.

CHAPTER
EIGHT

Charlie Payson was one of those small, slender blond men who could appear in a crowd and never be noticed. He had turned forty, but the gray at his temples was not noticeable, nor had the years been unkind to his thin sun-darkened face. He didn't look dangerous; neither was he belligerent. Which was why he had been picked for this job.

A harder man would have been noticed, and crowded — and judging by the caliber of the hardcases running Ladrone, would not have lasted two days.

But Charlie Payson rode into Ladrone on a droopy-headed piebald, a nondescript figure in a battered gray Stetson, a worn brush jacket, faded waist Levis tucked into scuffed half-boots, and even Skid Meskill, marshal of Ladrone, gave him only a cursory glance.

Charlie rode slowly up the dusty street until he came to the square, and the sun-warped bulk of the Come Again house blocked his path. He slid out of saddle, dropped reins over the tie pole, and stood a moment, considering his next move. He wore a star pinned to the inside of his shirt, and the authority of the United States backed that nickel symbol.

But until he found out what he had come to Ladrone for, he would be just another drifter, heading for Mexico.

He headed for the door, stepped meekly aside as a big, hard-faced man brushed past him, and went inside. The tall, bony, hollow-cheeked clerk behind the desk looked up as he approached.

"All filled up!" he growled, and then, as Charley hesitated, the clerk scratched the tip of his long thin nose, and suddenly shrugged. "Wait. Number ten's vacant. I forgot the fella who moved in yesterday won't be coming back."

Charlie said: "I ain't particular — long as he didn't have fleas." He signed the register, hesitating before writing down his name. The clerk's grin was sour. "That'll be a dollar in advance. You bring up yore own water, and you make up yore own bed."

Charlie paid him. He went out to fetch his warbag, and when he came back he noticed the clerk was reading an old newspaper. Charlie smiled. He found room ten, noticed the crumpled blankets on the bed, but no other sign of occupancy. Charlie was a meticulous man. He straightened out the blankets, straightened a faded print showing Indians charging across a plain, and then sat on a chair by the window and pulled a Missouri corncob from his jacket pocket. Charlie was not an impatient man. Unhurriedly he began stuffing tobacco into the bowl . . .

Johnny crossed the Mescalero and walked up Ladrone's hot main street. Marshal Meskill was just going into the

Casa Diablo, a saloon flanking a long shedlike structure bearing the title of Borderline Freight Company. The lawman stopped and scowled at the orphan, and Johnny grinned coldly as he went on up the street. The marshal made no move to intercept him.

Crossing the square, he went up the steps of the Come Again and walked through the lobby. The desk clerk looked up as he entered. Johnny ignored him as he went up to his room. He was thinking that he would be at loose ends until tonight — until he met Sally Ryan.

The door to his room was closed. He opened it and stepped inside. And then he slid aside almost instantly, his Colt sliding effortlessly into his fist. For a long, heavy moment he waited, eyeing the man in the chair by the window. The man had made no hostile move. He had a pipe between his teeth, and he was facing the door, and he didn't even look startled.

Johnny moved away from the wall then and kicked the door shut. "You one of the termites?" he asked coldly.

Charlie Payson looked puzzled.

"Who sent you up here?" Johnny snapped.

Payson shrugged. "You're ridin' up the wrong coulee, kid," he said. "No one sent me."

Johnny's quick glance took in the man's warbag by the bed. "Just moved in an' took over, eh?"

Payson's right eyebrow cocked. "I paid for the use of this room, kid. Cadaver downstairs said to take number ten, as the fella who had it before me wouldn't be coming back."

Johnny nodded understandingly. "Cadaver's a mite previous with his rooms, fella. I've come back." He looked at the bed; then his eyes met the mild gray eyes of the other. "An' I like to sleep alone," he said coldly.

Payson shook his head. "Cadaver said there wasn't another room in the house —"

"You argue that out with him," Johnny growled.

Charlie Payson got on his feet. He was wondering if this kid was the man he was to meet in Ladrone. He had expected an older man, but his instructions had been meager on this point.

"Sorry for this mixup, kid," he said calmly. "I'm Charlie Payson. Drifted into Ladrone this morning, an' I expect to be moving on by daybreak. I paid a dollar for this room an' I got a legal right to it. But —" he added quickly, seeing the danger signal flag up in Johnny's eyes — "I'm willing to toss you for it. Loser tries his luck somewhere else."

He had his hand in his pants pocket, and when he withdrew it he held a coin flat in his palm so that Johnny could see. It was a Mexican coin, notched with a triangular file!

Johnny's grin was crooked. "Yo're the second man who's volunteered to toss me for a place to stay. Funny thing, he pulled out the same coin, with the same notch in it. What is it — a fraternity?"

Payson shrugged. "I've been carrying this lucky piece around with me a long time, kid. If someone else has one like this I don't know about it."

"Well, mebbe you better hit him for a room, Charlie," Johnny suggested. "He's an old codger name of O'Leary — owns the livery stable on the edge of town, coming in from the desert side."

Charlie tossed the coin into the air and caught it, his palm covering it from Johnny's eyes. "You look like you'd take a gamble, kid —" he said quietly.

Johnny's eyes were suddenly cold. "Yore judgment's bad, Charlie. I gambled with O'Leary, an' he won. This time I'm stayin' — *an' yo're moving!*" He scuffed across the room to Charlie's warbag, eased his toe against it, and slid it across the floor to Payson. "*Take it, an' get out!*"

Stubbornness momentarily shouldered the mildness from Payson's thin face. Then he remembered that this youngster had given him the lead he wanted and that forcing trouble at this point would get him nowhere. He slid the coin back into his pocket, calmly tapped the contents of his pipe bowl into a cracked cup on the dresser. Then he picked up his warbag and walked past Johnny to the door, where he paused.

"You got that gun out pretty smooth, kid. But if I had been waiting for you, you'd never have reached the butt. Just remember that, while yo're in Ladrone, kid!"

He turned and closed the door behind him, smiling a little grimly at the look in Johnny's eyes. A wild kid, he thought. Probably got into some trouble an' headed for the Border. Wonder how long he'll last?

He went down into the lobby, carrying his warbag in one hand, his empty pipe between his teeth.

The hollow-cheeked desk clerk grinned uneasily as Payson walked to the desk. His Adam's apple bobbed nervously. "Leavin'?"

Charlie placed his warbag down carefully. He reached inside his jacket and brought out a walnut-handled Colt, which he placed on the counter, muzzle facing the hotel man.

"The other fella came back!" he stated calmly.

The clerk shrank away from the gun. He reached under the counter for the cash box and tossed a dollar toward Payson.

Charlie pocketed the money, slid the Colt out of sight, and picked up his warbag. "I wouldn't be around when that young bobcat comes down," he advised levelly. "He was plumb riled up when I left him."

The clerk watched Charlie go out. Then he shot a glance at the stairs, gulped, and ducked under the counter. He was taking Charlie's advice.

Johnny roamed restlessly around the room. The acrid aroma of Charlie's pipe irritated him and he pushed the sash up as high as it would go, stuck his head out of the window for a breath of fresh air. Then, remembering Charlie's parting advice, he frowned and pulled back into the room.

He had come into Ladrone with a chip on his shoulder, still smarting over the Rocking R's rebuff. He had loudly proclaimed why he had come to Ladrone to anyone who had listened, and now, as he looked back, he realized wryly that only the fact that the men running Ladrone had taken his coming lightly had kept him alive. Once they decided to get rid of him, he'd have to watch every alley, keep a wary eye on every man, sleep less easily.

He crossed to the bed and sat down. He had tipped his hand here, but that was before he had realized that the question of Lew Ferin's whereabouts was connected with a deeper game being played here in Ladrone.

Tando had said that "they" had killed Tennyson, even though the gambler was one of "them" because Tennyson knew Lew Ferin.

Irene had disclaimed knowing Ferin, even though Red had mentioned her name. Of course it might have been another Irene Red had referred to, but Johnny doubted it. And Irene had been running away when he had met her in the desert.

Johnny touched the bandages over his gash and grinned wryly. He had bulled around Ladrone without knowing what he was really bucking. But it occurred to him that if he had tipped his hand right from the start, he had also brought out into the open who "they" were.

He remembered the two men on the wagon in the desert. Skid Meskill's warning. Parks and Potsy. And the Mandells!

Johnny got up from the bed and walked to the scarred dresser. The face he saw in the dirty mirror had changed since the last time he had looked at it. It was a harder face, made grim by the bloodstained bandage over his eyes. It was thinner, too, and he looked older. He saw this in the eyes that looked back at him, and with a little shock he realized that the easy, careless humor that had been his armor against the world was gone.

He turned away, not liking what he had seen.

He looked at the bed, seeing Lew Ferin's squat, humorous face in his thoughts, and he said bleakly: "I don't know what this is all about, Lew. But if yo're still alive, I'll find you!"

He palmed the S & W again, checked it, replaced empty shells. That part of his equipment was in working order. Now he needed a cayuse and saddle. He spread the remains of last month's pay in his palm and was mildly surprised that his celebration back in Mesquite Junction had left him still with six dollars and six bits. Not enough to buy even a broken-down mount. But maybe O'Leary would let him hire an animal . . .

He left the room and went downstairs, passing through the lobby without thinking of the desk clerk. The square was deserted. A few hipshot horses nosed the rack in front of the Casa Diablo. The House of Prayer, across the street, was quiet, sulking under the midafternoon sun.

Johnny was turning away when he noticed two riders come out of the alley between the House of Prayer and the warehouse flanking it. They swung away from the square, and headed out of town. But Johnny had time to recognize both.

Irene Mandell and her edgy brother, Iron Mandell!

He watched them cross the wooden bridge past O'Leary's place, and their going irritated him without reason. He didn't like Iron Mandell's possessive attitude toward his sister.

The door of the House of Prayer opened and Clay Mandell came out. He stood on the board walk, watching Irene and his son, and even across the square Johnny sensed the rage in the man.

Wonder what's got him stirred up? Johnny thought.

The sky pilot seemed to sense Johnny's presence then. He turned and looked at Johnny, and the orphan swung around, not relishing another sermon from Irene's father. He heard the wagon rumble past, and dust swirled up and added its gritty film to the layers already deposited in the crooks and crannies of the weatherbeaten structures.

Johnny swung around and peered through the dust. He got a glimpse of the men riding the wagon seat and recognition knifed through him. This was the same wagon, and the same men, he had run into in the desert!

The wagon swung sharply into the alley leading to the Borderline Freight Company sheds. Johnny broke away from the walk. For the moment he forgot Irene Mandell. He had a score to settle with the two desert freighters, and that score came first.

Clay Mandell intercepted him. The sky pilot loomed up in the settling dust, a tall, black garbed figure with a peremptory voice. "Delaney!"

Johnny said sharply: "Sorry, Mandell. But I've —"

Irene's father caught him by the arm. "I've wanted to see you, since our misunderstanding," he insisted.

Johnny shrugged his arm free. "Some other time," he said impatiently. He started to move around Mandell, but the sky pilot blocked his path. "You're a stubborn youngster!" he snapped, and Johnny caught the anger in his voice now and he wondered if it was a carryover of the rage he had seen in the man.

"You can call it that, Mandell!" Johnny answered grimly. "But right now I've got a call to make. If you want to talk to me, I'm stayin' at the Come Again." He lifted his hand and pointed a finger at Clay. "Now get out of my way!"

For a moment Mandell's long, pious-looking face changed, revealed the naked murder behind the man's eyes. But he stepped aside. Johnny brushed past him, and broke into a run for the alley into which the wagon had disappeared.

He was too late.

A hostler was leading the unhitched wagon team toward a barn in the freight yard when Johnny intercepted him. He was a thin, oldish man with a worried look on his face.

"Where are they?" Johnny asked thinly. "The two men who just drove that wagon in here?"

"Pete an' Bunker?" the hostler said.

Johnny nodded. "Reckon they're the ones. Where'd they go?"

The other shrugged. "They checked in at the office, I reckon. If they ain't there, most likely you'll find 'em in some bar down the street. That desert crossin' is mighty dry, they tell me."

Johnny glanced toward the rear door leading to the freight line office. "They're gonna be a whole lot drier, if I find 'em," he muttered.

He crossed the yard to the loading platform, vaulted lightly up, and palmed a door open. He found himself in a dimly lighted room, and instinctively he palmed his S & W. There was light at the end of the room, and he walked to it.

A middle-aged man in shirtsleeves, standing by the door of a cubicle office, whirled around as Johnny came up. He saw the gun in Johnny's hand and he backed up against the door framing, his hands raising involuntarily.

"This a holdup?" he asked huskily.

Johnny holstered the S & W. "I'm lookin' for a couple of yore hands," he said bleakly. "Name of Pete — an' Bunker."

The other wet his lips. He was obviously a clerk, not in charge here. "They just left," he said. "You might find them in the Casa Diablo —"

Johnny moved on past him, out through the front door. He couldn't help thinking that Clay Mandell had delayed him just long enough to give Bunker and Pete a chance to lose themselves . . .

CHAPTER
NINE

Charlie Payson hesitated in front of the Come Again just long enough to give the impression of a bewildered man in search of lodging. He glanced up the road in the direction Johnny Delaney had said O'Leary's Livery Stables lay, shook his head, and walked to the rack where his piebald rolled its eyes and blew noisily. Charlie fastened his warbag to the saddle and started to climb aboard.

Skid Meskill came across the street then, a horny thumb hooked in his shell belt. The marshal's temper was edgy.

"You lookin' for somebuddy, stranger?"

Charlie turned and looked down on the lawman from his seat on the piebald. His glance jumped to the badge displayed prominently on Meskill's vest, and he seemed to shrink. "Just a bunk for tonight, Marshal," he said nervously. "I aim to be moving on in the morning."

Charlie's cowed manner seemed to soothe the marshal. "Too many strangers drift through Ladrone," he said loudly. "It's my business to check on all of them."

"I'm not looking for trouble," Charley said quickly. "Right now I'm on the move — I mean I'm out of a job," he amended weakly. "Riding chuck. But I'll move on, if you —"

"You can stay," Meskill said arrogantly. "I'm not bothered about a man's past — only his present business. While yo're in Ladrone, stranger, take this advice. Keep yore nose clean — an' yore eyes closed."

He turned on his heel, and Charlie watched the marshal strut away. Charlie smothered a small smile as he swung the piebald out into the street.

He rode at a slow jog until he came to the stables on the edge of Ladrone. The street narrowed to a brown ribbon of trail across the plank bridge, curling and vanishing in the hot brightness of the desert. He paused to look at that barren wasteland, wondering at the rapacity of men who would risk death in that waterless desolation a thousand times for money.

Then he turned the piebald into the stable yard and pulled up before the barn door.

O'Leary was on a bench in front of the office, reading a letter. He got up slowly, stuffing the letter into his shirt pocket. "Yep?" he queried.

Charlie looked him over. He saw a sawed-off man in baggy pants who seemed hard of hearing. A tobacco-stained beard stubble did little to hide the bitterness of his mouth.

Maybe this was the man, Charlie thought. But he had to be sure.

"I'm lookin' to bed Droopy here for the night," he said, sliding down from saddle. "He could stand a rubdown, an' a measure of oats to go with the hay."

"Leave him," O'Leary said surlily. "I'll take care of it."

Charlie nodded. "I'm a gambling man, O'Leary. I'll toss you for his grub and lodging — double or nothing."

O'Leary scowled. "I don't —" Then his gaze riveted on the coin Charlie was palming and he sucked in a small breath. Wordlessly he reached in his pocket and brought out the mate to that coin.

"Double or nothing!" he nodded.

They flipped, and O'Leary won. "Come inside," he invited.

O'Leary closed the door behind Charlie and waved him to a chair. "I've waited a long time for this," he muttered. He walked to a cupboard and took down a sealed bottle of whiskey. His fingers trembled as he broke the seal and poured. "What took you so long?" he rasped.

Charlie leaned back in his chair. "You didn't give us much to go on," he said. "It could have been the letter of a crank —"

O'Leary sneered. "I said I knew who and how, didn't I? You want the smugglers, don't you?"

Charlie nodded. "You didn't sign that letter we got at headquarters. Just this enclosed coin."

"I've got my reasons," O'Leary said. He took his drink neat and wiped his lips with his sleeve. "I want to make a bargain with you —"

"Charlie Payson," the U.S. marshal supplied. He sipped at his drink. "Not bad," he nodded, and finished it.

"Paid enough for it," O'Leary growled, refilling both glasses. "Ever hear of the Fallon boy? Convicted of train robbery? Governor turned down his pardon last year."

Charlie nodded.

"His real name is Thomas O'Leary," the oldster said. "He's my son!"

Charlie eased back in his chair. He held up his glass and eyed the whiskey speculatively. "What kind of a bargain, O'Leary?" he asked softly.

"I want a pardon for my boy," O'Leary said. "He was nineteen when they caught him in that holdup. Just a kid who fell in with a wrong crowd."

"Seems I remember that the engineer and the baggage-master were killed in that holdup," Charlie murmured.

O'Leary banged the table with his glass. "Tommy didn't have a hand in it. It was proved in court he was with the hosses. When it happened he was too scared to think. That's why he was caught. The top men got clear. The law had to hang the rap on someone, so they hung it on Tommy. If they could have proved he killed those men, he would have been hung!"

Charlie nodded sympathetically. "I'll do what I can. But I can't promise anything, O'Leary."

The oldster frowned. "You'll explain to the governor about this?" he asked. "You'll tell him who helped you?"

Charlie nodded. "If you help me break this gang up, I'll tell the governor. I think we can get him to review the Fallon case."

O'Leary got up and walked to the door. He threw it open and looked out into the stable yard. Charlie eyed him curiously.

"Thought I heard someone," O'Leary said. He turned and lowered his voice. "Ride down the river trail, Charlie. I'll saddle an' meet you somewhere along the road in a half-hour. We'll talk then."

Charlie nodded. He got up and walked to the door and stopped beside the older man. "I think we'll get the boy out," he said quietly, and went out into the yard.

O'Leary's lips moved soundlessly as he watched the U.S. marshal ride out of the yard and head for the river.

CHAPTER
TEN

O'Leary waited until Charlie was out of sight. Then he sagged down on the bench outside and pulled tobacco and pipe from his pocket. He had planned this a long time, gathering his evidence with the dogged patience of a man with one end in mind. He didn't gave a hoot about the men behind the crookedness in Ladrone. But he wanted his son out of jail, and for that he was willing to deal with Charlie Payson.

He let time slide by, while he smoked and let his thoughts range ahead to the day Tommy would be released. He'd sell out, he decided, and meet the boy in Austin. He'd saved enough money for him and Tommy to buy a small spread up north somewhere, and make a new start.

He finished his pipe and tapped the bowl against his heel. He got to his feet, feeling better than he had in five years. The stubble on his face itched, and as he scratched it he promised himself he'd shave regularly again.

He swung the big door open and walked into the barn.

The strong stable smells washed over him as he shuffled inside. But he was used to these and they made no impression on him. But a different odor, faint, yet unmistakable to his nostrils, stopped him. It was the odor of a cigaret, and O'Leary never used anything but a pipe.

He paused by the first stall, untenanted at the moment, and peered into the gloomier depths of the stable. His eyes had not yet accustomed themselves to the change from the bright sunlight, and he blinked suspiciously, a suddenly creepy feeling chilling him.

A horse moved restlessly in one of the stalls beyond. But there seemed to be no undue nervousness among the other animals. His own mare, a leggy sorrel, looked at him over the boards of its stall and whinnied a welcome.

O'Leary shrugged off his nameless fear. His eyes were adjusting to the interior and he could see nothing suspicious. He shuffled forward, his thoughts slipping back to the boy he had not seen in five years. His bridle was on a peg by the sorrel's stall, and he reached for it without thinking, habit directing his moves.

He didn't see the shadow slip out of the stall beyond and come toward him. He was holding the bridle in his left hand as he stepped in behind the sorrel and the animal suddenly moved, its hind quarters throwing O'Leary against the side of the stall.

O'Leary growled at the nervous cayuse. "What's got into yuh —"

He was partially turned, and he got a bare glimpse of the man before the heavy, long-handled pinch pliers crushed his skull. He collapsed against the stall side and fell face forward, half out of the stall. The killer

80

stood over him, the pliers in his hand, ready for another blow.

The sorrel was crowding the far end of its stall, shrilling nervously. The killer bent and saw that O'Leary was dead. He tossed the pliers aside and turned O'Leary over, so that the old man's face stared up at him.

The killer crouched and went through O'Leary's pockets. He found the notched coin, and with macabre mockery, he placed it on O'Leary's still lips.

The sorrel kept crowding the far end of the stall, even when the prowler had gone. Several times its soft whinny questioned the silent figure sprawled on the manure-dirtied floor, but O'Leary did not move.

Johnny came to O'Leary's stables a half-hour before sundown. He had spent his time in a fruitless search among the several saloons around the square, hoping to run into Bunker and Pete. But the men seemed to have vanished.

The shadows stretched across the stable yard as he paused in front of the combination office and sleeping quarters adjoining the barn. He wondered if the crotchety oldster would turn him down, his fingers jingling with the change in his pocket.

The barn door was wide open. He noticed this as he tried the office door, and when he found O'Leary wasn't in, he decided the oldster was probably going about some chore in the barn.

He walked in, his nose wrinkling at the strong barn smells. "Hello — O'Leary!" he called.

A horse whinnied a nervous answer. He frowned and moved toward the sound, his eyes slowly adjusting to the gloom. At that he nearly tripped over the body. He fell against the stall side, his hands slapping the boards with a hollow sound, and twisted fast, his left hand stabbing instinctively for his gun.

The silence was thick as death among the stalls. Out on the road a rider was approaching, the clip-clop of hoofs making a steady, rhythmic sound.

Johnny bent slowly over O'Leary's body. The pliers had made a mess of the right side of the old man's face, and Johnny gagged and cursed softly.

The rider turned into the yard. Johnny straightened quickly and stepped back into the darker end of the barn, his S & W ready in his hand. Whoever had killed O'Leary might be coming back . . .

The rider pulled up to one side of the open door, and Johnny heard him dismount, stand a moment, then try the office door. There was a long moment of silence, then the man's boots scuffed lightly in the yard, and a moment later a slight figure loomed up in the doorway.

The light was at the man's back, leaving his face dark and unrecognizable to Johnny, and he moved quickly. Johnny caught the faint glint from a gun muzzle as the newcomer palmed a weapon.

The orphan waited until the prowler came upon O'Leary's body. The man bent and after a moment gave a low, short whistle that held surprise and regret.

Johnny stepped out of the stall. "Drop yore gun!" he said bleakly.

The crouched man stiffened. But he was not fool hardy. He dropped his gun. And he made no other motion.

Johnny eased forward, and without surprise he recognized the crouched man. Charlie Payson, the man he had kicked out of his room in the Come Again House.

"Didn't think you'd go this far, Charlie," he said tonelessly. "Just to get a bunk for one night."

Charlie Payson's eyes were narrowed, the mildness gone from them. He looked hard and dangerous in this moment, and Johnny felt the change in this man. Drifter, nothing! he thought grimly, and though he had no liking for the oldster who had turned him out when he had needed help, he liked O'Leary's killer less.

"Too bad the law here's represented by a loud-mouthed phony," Johnny went on. "But I'm gonna see that Meskill jugs you for this —"

"You got a bad habit, kid," Charlie interrupted him coldly. "You jump to conclusions."

"Meanin'?"

"I came to see O'Leary, like you suggested. We talked. I rode out of town for a while. He was to ride out to meet me on the river trail. When he didn't show up, I rode back."

Johnny sneered. "Thought you didn't know **O'Leary**."

Charlie shrugged. He was looking into the steady muzzle of Johnny's S & W, and he debated with himself the wisdom of revealing his identity to this cold-eyed youngster. He didn't have much choice. This kid meant what he said. And he knew that once Skid Meskill

83

searched him, his marshal's badge would give him away.

"Sure, I knew O'Leary," he said. "Not by name. But he was expecting me. That's why I offered to toss you, kid. I was supposed to contact a man who had a coin that matched mine, and when you said O'Leary had such a coin I knew he was my man."

Johnny rubbed his stubbled jaw with the knuckles of his free hand. "Who are you then?"

Charlie said: "This'll explain." He eased his hand very carefully inside his jacket, unpinned his badge, and brought it forth. "Deputy U.S. marshal," he added. "O'Leary had evidence, and knew who was behind a smuggling ring operating out of Ladrone. He was going to tell me. But someone got him first."

Johnny eased back against the stall boards. "So that's why he offered to toss with me, that first day," he muttered. "When he saw I wasn't the man he was expectin', he was afraid to keep me here."

Charlie was eyeing Johnny with puzzled interest. "What's yore business in Ladrone, kid?" he asked.

"Cows," Johnny said thinly. "An' a friend of mine name of Lew Ferin." He gave a brief summary of why he had come to Ladrone. "Thought it'd be a lark, at first, Charlie. Ride in, find Lew, raise a little hell, like I was used to back in Mesquite Junction." He shook his head. "I haven't been too bright. But I'm beginnin' to think that Lew an' Red's comin' down here had somethin' to do with the rustlin' that's been strippin' the Rockin' R an' the Sleepy H."

Charlie nodded. He bent and picked up his Colt and eased it into his shoulder holster. "Looks like the same bunch is runnin' a two-way traffic across the desert. Chinks in — an' cows out!"

Johnny nodded. "All my leads have petered out. Except one." He glanced outside, where the fading rays of the sun made a blood-red pattern in the trampled dust.

"I came to see O'Leary about borrowin' a cayuse. But now —"

Charlie looked down at the small, crumpled body. "I reckon he won't mind, Johnny. Go ahead. I'll wait awhile, then drift back an' tell the town marshal that I found him like this."

Johnny bent over O'Leary, and Charlie helped him move the body away from the stall. The bridle lay where O'Leary had dropped it, and Charlie gave Johnny a hand with the saddle they found on a rack nearby.

The sorrel was skittish as Johnny led it out of the barn. He turned and watched Charlie come out to join him. "I've got an appointment down the river trail myself," he said. "I'll let you know anything I find out."

Charlie nodded. "From now on, I'd keep an eye on my back trail, son." He held out his hand. "Figgered you as a mite too cocky, back there in the Come Again, Johnny. I've changed my mind."

Johnny took the lawman's hand. "You didn't impress me, either," he chuckled. "But I'm glad we'll be workin' together on this."

Charlie stepped back as Johnny swung up into saddle. "Luck, son," he murmured, and Johnny raised his hand in a brief gesture as he swung the sorrel around.

CHAPTER
ELEVEN

Johnny came out to the street and looked back toward the square where the dying sun was making a bloody pattern against the sagging buildings. There were more horses tied to the racks, and more riders moving down the street, and Johnny had the feeling that Ladrone was beginning to come alive, shrug off the somnolence that the brutal midday sun imposed on it.

From the east a wind stirred, cool against his face, and it sighed over the flat, jumbled skyline that was Ladrone.

It was a strange moment for Johnny to think of Irene Mandell. But she came unbidden to his thoughts, stirring in him a feeling of anticipation that was almost eager.

Whatever her father and brother were, she was not part of it. He clung to this conviction with a strange stubbornness. The girl who had turned back in the desert to help him could not be hard — could not be part of the pattern he was beginning to see in Ladrone.

He had this girl in his thoughts, and he watched the tall figure of Pete, the whiskered gun guard on the wagon he had met in the desert, cross the street and go into the *Casa Diablo*, before recognition sank in, displacing Irene with a violence that sent him yanking at the sorrel's bit, his heels kicking the startled animal into a run.

He was out of saddle before the sorrel was within ten feet of the saloon rack, and he vaulted the tie bar, landing lightly on the raised walk in front of the Casa Diablo. The sorrel edged up to the rack and waited patiently, reins dragging.

A craggy customer with an early load on pushed through the batwings as Johnny moved for them. He teetered, blocking the orphan's path, and the cold-eyed youngster shouldered him roughly aside as he went inside.

The Casa was a low-ceilinged bar with pretensions. A huge oil painting of a Flemish nude was hung over the bar, which was of imported mahogany and finely polished. The liquor stock displayed on the shelves was varied and comprehensive, and the mirrors were remarkably clean.

But the quality of the customers lining the rail, or sitting at the scattered tables with the percentage girls, rated high only on the reward posters of a half-dozen states.

Johnny had been here earlier, at which time the Casa had been practically deserted. Now thick tobacco smoke lay like a slowly coiling sheath just below the ceiling, and the place was raucous with the sound of hard and strident voices.

The orphan paused just inside the doors, his glance moving among those men until he picked out the man he was after. Pete was standing at the bar, a tall pole of a man with his back to Johnny. A pearl-handled Colt jutted from a low-slung holster.

He was drinking alone, not talking to either of the two men siding him. Johnny pushed his way toward the bar, and men sensed the grim purpose in this youngster and edged away, their voices fading into a tense expectancy.

The tension spread to the men at the bar and one by one they turned, took a good look at the hard-eyed cowpoke from the Sleepy H, and edged away.

Pete did not turn around. But Johnny saw the man's eyes meet his in the mirror behind the bar. He was fingering his glass, and Johnny saw the shock of recognition burst in the man's blue eyes.

Even the bartender was crowding the far end of the bar, and Pete was alone, hunched over his glass.

Johnny's voice bit through the suddenly quiet room. "How's the chicken-freightin' business, fella?"

Pete didn't move — he didn't seem to hear Johnny. Just outside the door someone was calling for Meskill, his voice loud and urgent above the baited silence of the saloon.

Johnny shuffled forward, watching Pete's hunched figure. "It was a good shot," he said tonelessly. "But you should have made sure —"

He was less than three feet away from the man now, and Pete was lifting his glass as if to drink. The man's coolness was like a slap in the face to Johnny, and he reacted to it with almost fatal abruptness.

He took a quick step forward, intending to pull the man around. And in that moment Pete dropped his glass, slid sidewise along the bar, and whirled, his gun jerking into his hand.

Johnny spun around. Smoke wreathed his left hip as he drew and fired in a motion no one saw. He fired twice, the second report merging into the first.

Pete doubled up, turned half around, and fell on his Colt. The gun went off under him, muffled by his body.

Johnny was already heading for the door, his S & W covering every man in that smoke-filled room. Boots were pounding across the street. A man's voice, outside the batwings, said quickly: "In here, Marshal!"

Johnny whirled as Skid Meskill plunged through the batwings, gun in hand. He thrust out his foot, and the lawman tripped and fell across a table, collapsing it under his weight. Johnny backed to the wall to one side of the batwings and waited for the man who had called Meskill to enter.

He was short and squat, and he stuck his head and shoulders cautiously through the parted doors. Johnny reached out, grabbed a fistful of the man's shirt and hauled him inside. The man squawked and went for his gun, and Johnny laid the S & W across his bald spot and let him fall.

Meskill was scrambling to his feet. He was less than ten feet from the orphan when he fired his first wild shot. Johnny covered the distance in two jumps. Pete he had been forced to kill, but Meskill wore a badge, and Johnny respected that symbol from force of habit.

Meskill's second shot slammed into the floor as Johnny cuffed his hand down with his left and crossed his right in a savage hook for Meskill's jaw. The marshal's eyes glazed. Johnny jammed his S & W into Meskill's stomach, and hooked his right again to the lawman's jaw.

Skid Meskill hit the floor like a falling tree. He didn't even quiver.

Johnny stood over him a moment, his eyes challenging every man in that room. No one made a move.

A shred of the old Johnny stirred in him then. He knelt beside the marshal, reached under him for the badge he wore so prominently on his vest. The orphan's smile was bleak as he pinned the nickel symbol to the seat of Meskill's pants.

Straightening, he backed to the doors, paused a moment, then ducked out. No one moved until they heard a horse whirl and begin its run up the street. Then the frozen tension broke and talk surged through the room.

The bartender came up and pulled himself over the bar to look at Pete's huddled body. Then he turned and shook his head at the nearest man edging back to the counter.

"I've seen a lot of hard ones in the past ten years," he muttered. "But this kid —"

CHAPTER
TWELVE

The desert stretched out, bare and seemingly limitless, a scarred and broken land exposed to the naked glare of the sun. There was little beauty in it and less attraction, but Irene had found it comforting, and before she had tried the crossing she had often ridden out along the river trail, seeking in the arid and savage grandeur of the land an answer to the conflict within her.

Now she rode out again, but this time her brother rode with her. She had promised her father she would not try to run away, but Iron Mandell had insisted on accompanying her. Clay had tried to stop him, and the quarrel that ensued had driven Irene from the House of Prayer, to the stable which housed her mount.

Her brother had joined her before she finished saddling. He looked drawn and white, and she felt pity well up in her for this man who would always be unsure of himself.

She waited for him, and they rode out together, turning sharply for the trail at the end of town. Out of the corner of her eye she saw Johnny come out of the Come Again house, and she glanced quickly at her brother. But Henry was lost in thoughts he rarely expressed. Only the turmoil within him gave itself away in the fine beads of sweat on his forehead.

A trace of uneasiness made its way through Irene. But her brother seemed content just to ride with her, and once she was out of town, the loneliness of the land brushed over her with a soothing hand.

They rode for perhaps a half-hour before the trail swung in toward the river whose dry bed now lay a hundred feet below in a canyon it had eroded in chalk and limestone.

Irene reined in here and looked across the river, to Mexico — to low hills as bare and desolate as those on the American side. Her mother had died in Mexico, and Irene often wondered what had brought her mother here, and sometimes, with sudden shame, she wondered why her mother had married Clay Mandell.

Her brother edged his horse close and followed her gaze. And then, with bitter irony, he said: "You were happier in Mexico, weren't you?"

"I was younger," she answered, low-voiced. "I believed Father then, even admired him."

"And me?" he asked softly. "What about me, Irene?"

She turned, caught by the sense of strain, of almost bitter control, in his tone. "You were my brother — the boy I played with. We had fun, until —"

She paused, knowing how he felt about his hand.

He held up the claw, his thin face almost brutally distorted. "Until this happened!" he finished for her.

She didn't answer.

"*Wasn't it?*" he demanded harshly.

"You changed, after the accident, Henry," she said quietly. "No one could get close to you after that."

He laughed. It was thin and bitter laughter, and it marked him as nothing else did; it caused Irene to shrink from him. For there was a cruelty in it that drew from deep down in the man, from the hurt and frightened core of the boy she had known.

"I didn't change," he contradicted her. "But you did. Everyone changed. Even Clay." His voice shook with sudden passion. "I didn't care about them. Any of them. I hate them all. *All of them!*" he repeated.

"But you, Irene —" He reached out and gripped her bridle with his good hand. "I don't hate you, Irene."

Revulsion, pity and terror jumbled Irene's emotions and held her motionless. He looked into her face, as if searching for something, and suddenly he pulled her mount toward him and tried to encircle her waist with his other arm.

"I love you!" The words jerked from his tight lips, as if he expected them to be hurled back in his teeth. "From the day I found out you were not my sister —"

Irene pulled away from him, nearly spilling him. He regained his balance and cut his mount across her path, and laughed at her suddenly shocked and white face.

"Clay never meant for you to know!" he cried. "You were a year old when Dad married your widowed mother. My own mother had died, and Clay wanted someone to take care of me. I was four years old. Yore mother died a year later —"

Irene was looking at him as though he were a stranger. A phrase was repeating itself in her numbed head: "All these years —"

"Now you know," Mandell said. "Clay Mandell is your stepfather. There are no blood ties between us, Irene. Now you can see why I can tell you that I love you!" he said intensely. "Why I never let any man touch you! Not even Dad!" He laughed grimly. "I told him I'd kill him if he laid a hand on you, Irene —"

She backed her mount away from him. "All these years!" she said dully. "Torturing myself — hating myself for being Clay Mandell's daughter!"

He edged his horse close. "I'll take you out of Ladrone," he promised. "Soon as the next payment is made. And no one will stop me —"

"No!" She pulled away, and there was color in Irene's face.

Mandell's voice thickened. "That kid from up north? You picked him up in the desert! Why did you do it?" A wild jealousy was shaking him. "Is he the one you want?"

"For a human reason you'll never understand!" she lashed back. "He was hurt and needed help —"

But Mandell was beyond listening. "Is he the man?" he shouted. "*Answer me!*"

For answer Irene swung her mount around and touched spurs to flanks. The animal lunged ahead before Mandell could grasp the bridle. He yanked on his bit reins with cruel impatience and his mount suddenly balked. It sunfished and bucked, and Iron

Mandell had all he could handle in the next few minutes.

When he finally got the animal under control Irene was a speck on the trail to town.

Back in Ladrone Charlie Payson had waited patiently, giving Johnny time to ride out of town before reporting O'Leary's death to Marshal Meskill. He didn't know Johnny had headed for the Casa Diablo instead. The sudden breakout of firing from the square brought him out to the road. He saw Meskill running across the street for the saloon, disappear inside. There was another shot, a crashing from inside the saloon; then the squat man standing by the batwings pushed cautiously through the doors, only to suddenly jerk out of sight within.

Charlie frowned.

A few moments later Johnny appeared. He vaulted the rail, swung lithely up into saddle, and sent the sorrel running up the street. He saw Charlie standing at the entrance to O'Leary's stables, and he waved as he pounded past, heading for the river trail.

Charlie shook his head.

Men were converging toward the Casa Diablo, curious about the shots. Charlie drifted with them. A tall man in a black broadcloth suit shouldered him roughly on the walk. He didn't even look at Charlie. He was in a hurry, and the small cluster of the curious, grouped in front of the batwings, quickly opened up to let this man through.

Charlie moved slowly, a mild-eyed man who attracted no attention. He paused on the edge of the small group in front of the Casa Diablo in time to hear Meskill's anger-thickened voice: "Damn it, Clay, I couldn't stop him! The kid's dynamite, I tell you!"

The man he was talking to sneered: "He must be! Shoots Pete, buffaloes Bunker, and slaps you around as if you were a five-year-old. Got a sense of humor, too," the voice needled. "Maybe pinning that badge to the seat of your pants was where it belonged —"

"Aw — shut up!" Meskill snapped.

The batwings slammed open and Skid Meskill strode out, his face a dull red. He shoved the nearest man into the street, his temper a raw and ugly thing, and the others moved quickly out of his path.

Charlie moved to the edge of the walk. This was not the time to tell Meskill about O'Leary.

The marshal was headed past him, lips tight against his teeth, when he saw Charlie. He swung around to face Payson, his recent humiliation riding him, and in this mild, apparently harmless man he saw a chance to vent his rage.

"You!" he bit out. "What are you hangin' around for?"

Charlie swore silently. This was the last thing he had wanted. Ladrone's lawman was just riled enough to take his anger out on the first man to cross him.

"I —" He hesitated, backing away a little from the man looming over him. "I was looking for you, Marshal."

The batwings creaked again as the tall man who had passed Payson on the walk a few minutes before stepped outside. He paused and looked at Charlie, and Payson caught the sudden suspicion that flickered into the man's pale, cold eyes.

Meskill was breathing down on Charlie, his voice thick and menacing. "What'd you want to see me for?"

"He's a friend of the kid's," someone in the crowd spoke out. "I saw the younker wave to him as he rode out of town, Skid."

The tall man came to stand beside Meskill. "Another stranger in town, Skid. Another sinner come to foul our town. Marshal, the salvation of repentant sinners is my task. But the enforcement of law and order is yours. If this man is that young scoundrel's partner, then it is your duty —"

"Just a minute, preacher," Charlie interrupted coldly. "I never saw that kid until I came to Ladrone."

Mandell looked over the crowd. "You saw the kid wave to this man, Stiles?"

Stiles emphatically repeated his statement.

Charlie looked around him. The rough crowd would give him no quarter. But he clung to the role he had assumed, hoping to ride this situation out. He was not yet ready to tip his hand, knowing that once he revealed himself as a Deputy U.S. Marshal he would never find what he had come after.

"I saw the kid ride by," he nodded. "I had just come out of O'Leary's —"

"What were you doing in O'Leary's place?" the tall man asked quickly. He had taken over from Meskill, assuming an authority the marshal did not question.

Charley shrugged. "I rode in to put up my cayuse."

"Get O'Leary here!" Mandell ordered the man nearest him. "We'll find out if he's telling the truth!"

The man broke away from the crowd and headed for the livery stables. Charley's lips felt dry. This sky pilot was a phony. He knew O'Leary was dead! Charley saw that knowledge in the man's eyes.

"O'Leary won't be here!" he said grimly. "O'Leary's dead!"

The tall man smiled. A growl went through the crowd. Meskill made a small sound in his throat.

"He was dead when I rode in," Charlie said. "Someone crushed his skull. Maybe with a gun barrel. I was just coming to tell you, Marshal, when the commotion broke out —"

"Every sinner has an alibi, Skid," Mandell interrupted dryly.

"Get a rope!" someone shouted from the rear of the gathering crowd. "Let's string the dirty killer up!"

"I'll handle this!" Meskill growled. "If Tim comes back an' says O'Leary is dead, we'll —"

The clatter of a hard-running horse suddenly broke upon the quiet of the square. Involuntarily men turned to see, and that momentary lapse gave Charley his chance.

His hand flicked inside his unbuttoned jacket. Meskill didn't even see the gun muzzle as it jammed into the already sore area above his belt. It drove the breath out of him in one great whoosh. He doubled, and Charlie shoved him into Mandell, and made a break down the walk. He had almost reached the alleyway that broke the solid building line when a gun boomed. The slug slammed Charlie forward. He fell on his knees and the second bullet screamed over his head. He lurched erect, his left side numb from the shock of the bullet, and fell back against the building corner.

At bay, he emptied his gun into the crowd, sending them scurrying for cover. Then he lurched around the corner, into the alley, and started to run. But his legs were weak and each dragging breath seemed to burn in his side.

The rider came down the alley. The sun had gone down behind the Ladrones, but there remained enough light to show Charlie that the horseman was a girl! He turned, bringing up his Colt, and only then remembered it held no live shells.

Irene Mandell dismounted beside him. "I don't know who you are!" she said hurriedly. "But take my horse and get away from here. Hurry!"

He was too sick to ask needless questions. "Thanks, ma'am," he muttered as he heaved himself up. "Some day, maybe, I'll —"

She slapped the animal's rump. "Ride!" she said sharply. And as the animal leaped away, she added brokenly: "And may God be with you!"

Iron Mandell rode into town fifteen minutes behind Irene. He had not tried to catch up with her, preferring to be alone with his bitter thoughts. He found Ladrone strangely stirred, buzzing with an excitement above the usual nightly celebration.

But Ladrone's inhabitants had learned through experience that this Mandell preferred to be left alone. So it was that Iron rode up the street to the House of Prayer and went inside without an inkling of what had happened.

He walked through the big empty room with its benches and pulpit, where his father daily thundered at sin and wickedness, and went directly to the big living room in the rear.

Clay Mandell was sitting behind a small mahogany desk. Meskill was sitting on a horsehair sofa, holding his head in his hands. He looked sick. A half-dozen craggy hombres stood around uneasily.

Iron Mandell slowly closed the door behind him. His bright gaze took in those sullen men, lingered coldly on Meskill.

"What's wrong with him?" he asked unsympathetically.

Clay sneered. "First that kid, Delaney, made a monkey out of him. Big, tough Skid Meskill!" The marshal writhed under the harsh taunt, but he did not lift his head.

"Then, just a few minutes ago, the kid's partner, half Meskill's size, gives him a bellyache with five inches of gun muzzle —"

"Kid's partner?" Iron interrupted, frowning.

His father nodded. "We figured it was the kid O'Leary was waiting for. But I think we were wrong. Bunker says he's sure it was this other fella who left O'Leary's place, just before Bunker killed the old fool."

Bunker nodded. The squat man was hiding an egg-sized lump under his hat. "I heard O'Leary call this jasper Charlie when he rode away. I was waiting in the barn. O'Leary sat out on his bench a heck of a long time before he came inside." Bunker grinned sourly. "He never knew what hit him."

Iron Mandell shrugged. "It was bound to come," he muttered. He reached in his coat pocket for one of several cigarets he had rolled himself earlier in the day. He wouldn't ask anyone to roll a smoke for him, and his pride refused to let any man see his painstaking, fumbling attempts which he essayed only in the strict privacy of his room.

"What's happened since I left?" he asked thinly.

Clay Mandell filled in details. "The kid got away, right after killing Pete. But one of the boys wounded his partner. If it hadn't been for Irene, he wouldn't have gotten away!"

"Where is she?" Iron asked bleakly.

"Locked in her room!" Clay answered. He got to his feet, kicking his chair back, and his face was grim as he looked at his son. "What happened between you two?" he demanded. "What did you tell her?"

"The truth!" Iron Mandell answered meagerly. He met his father's anger with a cold, unblinking stare that warned Clay, throttled his anger before it got out of hand. This dark-faced, moody man was his son — yet Clay knew that Iron would kill him as easily and with as little emotion as he had killed the dozen others who had gotten in his way.

"From now on, she'll stay in her room," Clay said harshly. "She'll go out only when I'm with her —"

"No!" Iron's voice was so soft it barely carried to Clay. But it was as authoritative as a whiplash. "Let her out!"

The elder Mandell stiffened. Even Meskill sensed the sudden threat of violence in that room. He raised his head and stared, muddy-cheeked, at the slim man with the claw hand.

"Delaney'll be back," Iron Mandell said. "He'll be back for Irene — and I want her to see him!"

Clay Mandell nodded. This was what he had wanted, what he had intended for Iron Mandell. There wasn't a more deadly man than his son. But he never took orders. Clay knew if he had told Iron to gun Johnny, his son might have balked.

"Handle it your way," he agreed. "But don't underestimate him, son. Pete was no slouch with a Colt. And from what I hear he had the jump on the kid. Yet he barely cleared holster."

Iron Mandell's smile was like a cat's, lazily cruel.

"I'm sending Bunker up to Canyon Verde," Clay said. "The other herd's due any time now. But I want Parks back in town." He glanced at Meskill, and his lips twisted. "I don't think Skid's going to be of much use to us any more."

Meskill's shoulders sagged, but he made no reply.

Bunker looked at Clay. "I'd better get ridin'," he suggested.

Clay nodded. "And don't forget to tell Evans to get rid of Ferin. Those are orders!"

Bunker nodded. "I'll tell him."

CHAPTER
THIRTEEN

Johnny Delaney rode south along the river road, in the direction opposite to that taken by Irene and Iron Mandell earlier in the afternoon. The stony aridity of the desert petered out here. Clumps of cottonwoods began to appear where the stream made a wide bend and headed into Mexico between high bluffs.

Two miles out of Ladrone, Johnny slowed down. He remembered he was to look for a Joshua tree, and with the evening shadows beginning to slide long and purple from the hills, he didn't want to miss it.

For Sally Ryan was his last hope. So far he had gotten nowhere in his search of Ferin. Lew had come to Ladrone — and disappeared! Red Tanguey had come back with a bullet in his lungs!

More strongly now Johnny was convinced there had been more behind Red and Ferin's trip to Ladrone than the casual jaunt it had seemed. Rawline, the Rocking R owner, had been getting desperate over the rustling of his stock. His uncle, Andy, had complained less — but Johnny knew that the Sleepy H had been losing stock too.

Johnny frowned. Charlie Payson had mentioned a two-way traffic from Ladrone — cattle and aliens.

Who was behind it? Was the House of Prayer a cover behind which the Mandells directed operations?

He remembered the strange noises that had come from within the wagon driven by Bunker and Pete. Chinks — being freighted across the desert under cover of night to some distribution point up north. And he remembered how Clay Mandell had held him up when Pete and Bunker had come back to Ladrone.

He had figured Clay Mandell as a phony, right from the first meeting. But he was Irene's father, and the fact bothered him. Whatever was due to break, he didn't want to hurt her.

He was thinking of her as he rode past the Joshua tree. It grew just off the river side of the road, its limbs twisted and flattened as if in supplication over the stream bed.

He would have gone further if the woman's voice, a frightened whisper, hadn't reached him. "Señor Delaney?"

He swung his animal around and rode back, seeing only a shadowy figure sitting on a horse under the tree.

"Mrs. Ryan?"

"Tando said you'd be here earlier," the woman said. She had a soft, yet somewhat harsh voice.

Johnny nodded. "I was unexpectedly detained, Mrs. Ryan."

"You can call me Sally," the soft voice requested. She rode out of the shadows and Johnny saw a dark-skinned, smiling woman who must have been beautiful ten years before. But thirty had begun to sit rather hard on Sally — she had broadened and thickened in the wrong places. The lines in her face, mostly about her eyes, were inevitable — but when she smiled she recaptured much of the beauty that had made her the toast of Ladrone.

"Tando said you were a friend of my husband," she went on, looking him over, "but I hardly expected to find a boy."

Johnny smiled. "I'm past the age of mothering, Mrs. Ryan."

"Sally," she corrected him teasingly. "Sometimes my husband called me his 'Lady of Shalot.' He was a strange man, my husband. A gambler — a restless man. Did you know him well, señor —"

"Call me Johnny," the orphan supplied gallantly. "No, I didn't know yore husband. But a friend of mine did. Lew Ferin."

"Yes, I remember," Sally said. "But I thought you —" She faltered, and Johnny saw disappointment push the smile from her face. "My husband, Tennyson, is dead," she continued stiffly. "He was killed because he knew Lew Ferin."

"Did they kill Lew, too?" Johnny asked softly.

"I don't know," Sally replied. Her voice was bitter. "But if he had not come to Ladrone, my husband would still be alive. The fools!" she hissed. "They thought my husband was doublecrossing them — was giving information to this man Ferin. So they killed him."

"Who are they?" Johnny asked grimly.

"The Mandells!" Sally said harshly. "They run Ladrone, Johnny. My husband worked with them. Your friend Ferin met him in the Casa Diablo. They talked over old times. There was another man with him — red hair, tall —"

Johnny nodded. "Red Tanguey. He died in Mesquite Junction, after riding across the desert with a bullet in his lung."

Sally shook her head. "They killed my husband that same day they shot this Red. It was Parks who killed him. They brought him home to me. I did not cry. Like the wife in the book, Johnny — I could not cry. And I did not die."

She smiled again suddenly, and held out a small book, bound in black leather worn to chamois softness by much handling. "Often he read to me from this book, Johnny. Beautiful words — sometimes they made me cry. Do you like poetry?"

Johnny thumbed the leather cover open. The Poems of Alfred, Lord Tennyson. Across the flyleaf, written with a delicate woman's hand, was penned: *To Paddy, who will never grow up. Kate.*

"He was good to me, Johnny," the woman said. "Many times I did not understand all that he talked about. Often he drank. And when he was drunk — then he did not want me near. But always he was good to me."

Johnny thumbed through the book. Some of the verses were underlined. He was about to close the book when a scrawled map on the back cover caught his eye. There was Ladrone in the lower left-hand corner, a stream that seemed to vanish against wavy lines that were meant to be hills, and beyond them, ringed by these lines, a space marked Canyon Verde.

"Canyon Verde," Johnny said aloud. "Did he ever mention this to you, Sally?"

The woman nodded. "That is where the cattle, stolen from up north, are rebranded. Then they are driven down into Mexico, and sold."

"Nice setup," Johnny muttered.

"That is where Parks and Potsy went," Sally said. "I saw them ride toward the hills. They must be expecting more cattle in Canyon Verde, Johnny. Always, when Parks and Potsy leave Ladrone and ride toward the hills, they go to Canyon Verde."

Johnny closed the book. "I'd like to keep this, Sally. For a while."

The woman laid a hand on his arm. She was close to him then, but the shadows were thickening and they were kind to Sally. "There are many of them, Johnny. Bad men who will kill anyone who gets in their way. I think your friend, Lew Ferin, was taken to Canyon Verde. Why, I do not know. But it is foolish for you to go there. Alone. I have told you what I know. Ride back across the desert and get help. Bring many men with you, Johnny —"

"I have help," Johnny said thinly. "A man named Charlie."

"One man?" Sally said. She shook her head. "You do not realize —"

"We'll handle it!" Johnny interrupted her. "Thanks for the information." He pulled away from her before she could speak. "I'll wait here until you get out of sight, then follow."

She remained still, not moving. "Johnny!" she whispered. Then, without waiting for him to answer, she turned her pony and sent it back along the trail to Ladrone.

Sally Ryan rode toward Ladrone, whose lights were beginning to pin point the gathering dark. She had come to this meeting at Tando's request, and because she wanted to hurt the men who had killed her husband. She rode back now, tired and strangely depressed. She had known men before Tennyson, but only he, of all of them, had been kind to her. Long after she had begun to fade he had kept alive in her the feeling of being beautiful, of being desired. His death had taken these props from her and, like a little girl she alternated between depression and joy.

Meeting Johnny had confused her. He was young, and in his presence she had felt the weight of her years, the nights that stretched behind her — she had felt so much older than this boy, and motherly. And yet vanity had moved her, too — a vanity that denied she was ten years older than Johnny. She needed the reassurance that Tennyson had given her — the reassurance that she was young, she was beautiful, she was vital — and she would live like that forever.

A reassurance no man would ever give her again.

The lights of Ladrone shone across the bend in the river, and caution stirred through the disturbed thoughts of Sally Ryan. It suddenly occurred to her that she had been rash in meeting this young stranger. For the Mandells and their crowd ran Ladrone, and though Tando was a power across the Mescalero, still the Mandells would not hesitate to smash the Toreador if they thought Sally Ryan had betrayed them.

She rode past the bridge crossing and beyond it for two miles before swinging the bay toward the river. She knew this country like the back of her hand, and she guided the bay across the shallow river, picked up a faint trail beyond and swung back toward the Ladrone.

She was moving at a canter when her bay suddenly shied. A shadow loomed up before her and she caught the faint glint of light from a raised weapon. An involuntary cry tore from her throat, and instinctively she threw up her arms to shield her face.

A man's voice, clipped hard, said: "Sorry, ma'am. I thought — you were someone else —"

She put her hands down on her pommel as her bay snorted nervously. Close up the shadow resolved itself into a slight man riding bent over in saddle. He looked small and mild and definitely not dangerous.

"Bad night for — a woman — to be riding around," he said brokenly, and Sally knew then that he was hurt. Even as she sensed this, he sagged forward. His gun slid out of his hand and thudded into the loose sand under the horse's feet.

She edged the bay alongside him and put a hand on the man's arm. Her eyes had become accustomed to the night, and the Border stars blazing in the clear sky provided illumination enough for Sally to see that this man was a stranger to her. He had a thin, dark face that

111

was not young nor yet grooved by the years. He didn't look as if he had a peso to his name, and it occurred to her that this man might be a new addition to the Mandell crowd. The thought stiffened her, and she jerked her hand back.

The man's voice essayed a chuckle. "I'm harmless — ma'am. Won't — bite —"

She steadied him as he sagged over the pommel. "Who are you?" she asked.

"Charlie," he said faintly. "Name's Charlie —"

Charlie? He was the man Johnny Delaney had mentioned. Sally Ryan made a quick decision.

"Hold on!" she encouraged. "I'll get you to where you'll be safe. Get you a doctor —"

Charley nodded. His fingers curled around the saddle horn. The slug in his back, narrowly missing his lung, had made him bleed a lot. He had been riding aimlessly for the past hour, and now he gritted his teeth, holding onto his fading consciousness with grim will.

Sally Ryan grasped his mount's bridle. "Hold on!" she repeated. And with Charlie in tow, she swung down the faint trail toward the Toreador.

CHAPTER
FOURTEEN

Johnny rode back to Ladrone less than ten minutes behind Sally. Unlike Sally, he was not disturbed by thoughts of the years behind him, nor of those immediately ahead. This meeting had provided the one lead he had been looking for — he knew why Lew Ferin had come to Ladrone. And unless Sally Ryan was wrong, where he had been taken.

Canyon Verde!

At the bridge crossing into Ladrone, he pulled up, realizing suddenly that after what had happened in the Casa Diablo, Ladrone would no longer be safe for him. The Mandells would be out to get him now, indirectly perhaps, behind the guns of some hireling. Or Skid Meskill would take his opportunity from the shelter of some dark alleyway, relying on his badge to carry him through whatever questioning would follow.

It would be wiser if he rode for Canyon Verde now. This was what he had come after — to find Lew Ferin.

But Charley Payson would be waiting for him — wanting to know what Sally Ryan had revealed. And as he hesitated he thought of Irene Mandell, and suddenly he knew he had to see her. He had forced her to ride back here, and he could not avoid his responsibility to

113

her. Whatever the Mandells were, Irene was not one of them.

Instinctively he loosened the S & W in his holster as he turned the sorrel across the heavy planking and rode on into Ladrone.

Lamplight splattered the street leading to the square where the Come Again loomed its dark bulk against the sky. Johnny rode past the dark alleyway leading to O'Leary's Stables, and he wondered what explanation Charlie had given Meskill.

There were more horses lining the saloon rails, and some rigs, a few broken down, sagging wagons. But there were few men on the walks. No one noticed Johnny as he rode toward the square, heading past the Green Dragon. He had not foreseen the shootout in the Casa Diablo when he had left Charlie, and thus had prearranged no meeting place. He would have to rely on information casually picked up at the nearest bar . . .

He saw the girl out of the corner of his eye, walking swiftly across the street. He knew that walk, thought he had seen her walk only once — walk with her brother and father out of the Green Dragon. There was something prideful about it, a head-up erectness that caught the eye and stirred interest.

Johnny slid quickly out of saddle, dropped the sorrel's reins over the nearest pole bar, and intercepted Irene Mandell just as she turned to the Green Dragon. He didn't see the man who had been watching her from the shadows across the street, nor did Johnny notice that this man turned on his heel, a tight grin on his face, and hurried to the House of Prayer.

"Irene!" he called, and she whirled. He saw the gladness in her face, and it stirred a responsive warmth in him. He could not remember any woman being glad to see him — not the way this girl looked — and in that moment Johnny Delaney crossed the threshold into maturity.

"Johnny!" she cried softly, and her fingers dug into his arm. "Johnny — take me away from here!"

He glanced back up the street. "I promised you that, Irene," he said. "But first I've got to see a man named Charlie Payson —"

A door slammed in the House of Prayer. Irene heard it and shrank back against the Green Dragon door. "In here, Johnny," she whispered. "They let me out to have dinner. We can talk — in here!"

He pushed open the door for her. The transition was easier at night, and he knew what to expect. And with this girl at his side, pressing against him, he felt older and more sure of himself.

He was prepared for Sun Yat Sen this time. "Rear booth," he said quietly, and stared levelly into Sen's bland face.

He let Irene order for both of them. She ate here often, she said, and knew the menu. He smiled. "If you like the grub, I reckon I can give it a try."

He eased back and watched her. She seemed to relax in the intimacy of the booth, the tenseness leaving her shoulders. She was wearing the brown taffeta dress that did not become her and a black, shapeless hat she unpinned from her hair and set down on the seat beside her. Dress and hat made her look older than her nineteen years, and Johnny wondered if Clay Mandell, for some obscure reason, was trying to punish his daughter.

Her hair was bunned on her neck, drawn smooth over her ears, and the candle on the table picked up the dark red streaks in it. Her face was small, fine and well moulded, and whatever the background of this girl, something had shaped character in her, forged it on the anvil of her will.

She caught his steady glance as she raised her eyes, and red flushed across her cheeks.

"You know," he said a little awkwardly, "I never had a good look at you."

She recovered composure more quickly then he did. "I don't mind," she said.

He grinned. "I'm glad it was you who ran into me in the desert." He saw her eyes grow troubled, and he added seriously: "I didn't realize what I was making you do, Irene. I could have as easily ridden back to Mesquite Junction with you. But I had started out for Ladrone —"

"Why?" the girl interrupted. "Why did you come here — alone?"

"Stubbornness, I guess," he answered. "And to find out what had happened to Lew Ferin."

He told her about himself, and what had happened in Mesquite Junction. "I started out to prove to Sheriff Marasek and the others back there I wasn't just a wild kid. I almost didn't make it." He was silent as the waiter brought their order.

Impulsively Irene put her hand on his, across the table. "Johnny — get out of Ladrone. Leave it to other men to handle — men whose business —"

"Finding Lew is my business, Irene," he said stubbornly. "And I promised Charlie Payson I'd tell him what I found out. I —"

The girl shook her head. "Charlie is dead, Johnny. He was badly shot up a few hours ago."

"Why?" Johnny's voice was grim.

She told him how she'd help Charlie get away. "They claim he killed O'Leary. But I didn't know that when I rode down into that alley and gave him my horse. He could barely stand. But he got away."

"He didn't kill O'Leary," Johnny said bleakly. "Charlie Payson is a U.S. marshal, Irene. O'Leary was going to tell him who was behind the smuggling and the rustling in this part of Texas. I found out what O'Leary knew —" He paused, looking directly at the girl across the table. He was going to hurt her, but he had to tell her.

"Yore father and brother run Ladrone," he said levelly. "The Mandells — the pious soul-savers of Ladrone!"

She looked at him, her face white. "I know," she said softly. "I've known — for a long time. At first I didn't want to believe it. Then I couldn't stand it. That's why I ran away. O'Leary helped me that first time."

Johnny nodded. "I'm glad you know. And I'm sorry it's yore father and brother mixed up in this."

117

She shook her head. "I found out something today, Johnny — something that's made it easy to break away. I found out that —"

"Found out what, Irene?" the thin voice questioned.

Irene gasped. Johnny swung around and faced the man who had come noiselessly down the aisle to stand before them.

"What have you found out?" Iron Mandell repeated. His dark face had a wild congestion. "*That I love you! Is that what you found out today, Irene?*"

Johnny came to his feet, slowly. He felt crowded and trapped in the narrow confines of that booth. For a brief instant he had the dismal thought that if Irene had wanted to trap him she could not have picked a better spot. And then, almost instantly, he rejected it.

There was fear in her face, and disgust — and her voice cut at this man she had called brother with bleak contempt. "So that's why you forced Father to let me out! So you could follow me, spy on me!"

Johnny's gaze flicked past Mandell to the three men waiting farther up the aisle. He recognized Clay Mandell — the other two he did not know.

Iron Mandell's voice was wild. "I would have killed him, if he had told me you were seeing this — this range bum! I would have killed any man who dared hint you were the cheap —"

Irene stood up and slapped him. The sound was like a report in that hushed stillness. It rocked Iron Mandell back, and turned him into a savage beast. He swung his claw hand for her face, and only Johnny's lunge saved her from mutilation. The three-pronged claw grooved deep into the booth wall.

Mandell's right hand dipped inside his coat. He was fast, but his very rage trapped him. In that moment he wanted to kill Irene Mandell more than he wanted to kill Johnny — he lunged back to cut down at her, standing frozen against the booth side.

Johnny shot without thinking.

His slug doubled Iron Mandell. The report hammered through the dining room; then Iron's gun went off. He was unhinging at the knees, falling forward, and he kept pulling trigger until he fell.

Johnny turned to Irene. A shot splintered wood a foot above his head. Through it all Irene hadn't moved — he couldn't tell if her brother's shots had hit her. A second bullet smashed china on the table, and Johnny moved, risking his life in a break out of that booth. Those men up the aisle were shooting for him, but they had no regard for the girl with him.

He stumbled over Iron Mandell's body, fell against the opposite booth, and cut loose at Clay and the others with the remaining shells in his S & W. It drove them to cover among the booths, and gave him time to reach the back door. He shoved through it into the kitchen where a steamy variety of smells almost choked him. A Chinese cook was backed against the wall, a cleaver held in his upraised hand.

Johnny ran past him to the door and found himself in an alley. He stumbled over garbage cans, regained his feet, and started for the street. Men appeared in the alley mouth, moving cautiously.

Johnny cursed silently and doubled back. He paused briefly to slip fresh shells into his gun, and this delay gave one of the men from the Green Dragon time to reach the back door.

Johnny saw the shadowy form move against the light from the kitchen — a tall, rawboned man with a gun in his hand. Johnny was clearing the overturned can when the man stepped out. They collided, but Johnny had the advantage of having glimpsed the man, and he used his shoulder to jam the man back against the door framing.

The man cursed and tried to bring his gun hand up. Johnny chopped his own weapon across the man's forearm, and the other gave a sharp cry as he dropped his gun.

A .45 blasted from inside the kitchen. Whoever was shooting wanted Johnny's hide badly; and he wasn't counting the risk to his own man. Johnny heard the bullet splat into the rawboned man's side. The man grunted, as if the wind were knocked from him.

Johnny broke away from the revealing back door light. He caught a glimpse of Clay Mandell steadying himself for another shot, and he whipped his arm across his chest and slammed a shot into the room. He didn't expect to hit Clay, and he didn't. But the slug, whanging into an iron pot hanging beside Mandell, spoiled the sky pilot's aim.

Johnny legged it down the alley. He ended up against a high board fence that walled off the warehouse yard. He turned. Men were running down that alley now, some of them shooting indiscriminately into the darkness. Mandell's voice was raging. "Five hundred dollars to the man who gets him! He killed my son! Damn his black soul! Get him alive and I'll make it a thousand dollars!"

Johnny swung back to the barrier. He snugged his S & W into his holster, took five long strides, and jumped. His fingers closed over the top of the fence and he hauled himself up in one quick, smooth motion. For a brief moment he was outlined against the stars, and a bullet whispered an unfriendly message past his ear.

Then he dropped into the blackness of the warehouse yard.

Fifteen minutes later he was crouched under the south bank of the river that ran past the desert end of town. Men were combing the yards behind the Green Dragon, spurred by Clay Mandell's reward offer.

For the first time since Iron Mandell had confronted him and Irene in the restaurant, Johnny had time to think. Irene's brother had come to kill him, to kill her! He had come not as a brother, but as a jealous lover — and behind him, obviously backing Iron's move, had been Irene's father!

Of this Johnny could make little sense. He had killed Iron Mandell, and what effect this would have on Irene, he could not even guess. But as he crouched there in the temporary protection of the river bank, he knew this was more important to him than finding Lew Ferin.

He had to see Irene Mandell again.

A sliver of moon rose late that night. The stars made their slow wheel in the midnight sky, and slowly the commotion subsided in Ladrone as man after man gave up the search for Johnny Delaney.

In those hours the orphan played a fantastic game of hide and seek. But he found no trace of Irene Mandell.

He came to O'Leary's, a grim and silent shadow, intending once more to borrow a horse from the stables. O'Leary, he felt sure, would not mind.

He came slipping quietly down the alley, and he smelled the man's cigaret before he saw him. His smile was tight-lipped. They knew he needed a mount to get away, and they were overlooking no bets.

He waited in the shadows with the patience of a stalking Apache. He heard the man move, scuff his boots on the packed earth. A glowing butt arced into view and scattered its tiny sparks on the stable yard.

The man swore half-heartedly. He walked into view, a stooped, thin man with bowed legs. He was carrying a rifle. He paused in front of the open barn door, peered into the pitch darkness. A horse stamped restlessly on wooden planking within.

"Think he'll come around here, Teeter?" the stooped man questioned.

A grunt floated out of the barn.

The guard repeated the question, waited patiently, then shrugged. He turned and walked back out of Johnny's sight. The bench creaked as he deposited his slight frame on it.

Johnny frowned. *Two of them!* The one on the bench he could dispose of — but Teeter would give him trouble.

He bent, felt around until he had gathered a handful of pebbles. He drew his S & W and held it ready in his left hand.

With a quick sidearm motion he scattered the pebbles down the alley.

They made a soft, skittering sound in the dark. Johnny crouched and meowed softly. He made the sound urgent, throaty.

The bench creaked. There was a tense moment of quiet, and Johnny could almost see the stoop-shouldered guard peer toward the alley. He meowed again, and with his fingers he scratched his pants leg.

Boots scuffed cautiously. The guard came into view, his rifle held across his thin frame. "Teeter!" he called anxiously. "You hear that?"

If Teeter heard, he kept his silence. The guard hesitated. Johnny soundlessly gathered up several more pebbles. He threw them behind the guard, and simultaneously his meow changed to an outraged yowl.

The startled guard jumped. He turned, poking his rifle toward the sound, and Johnny came up behind him in three long strides. He brought the S & W down in a quick chop across the man's skull and then caught him as he slumped.

Carrying the man to the bench, he eased him down upon it. Johnny hesitated. There was no sound from inside the barn, other than the occasional restless thumping of one of the stalled animals.

He meowed softly this time and kept it up as he eased toward the barn door, hugging the side of the barn. Then he cut it off short, and after a moment he whispered: "Teeter! Did that fool cat go in there?"

Whoever Teeter was, he was either very cautious, or he was distrustful of the man who had been delegated to stand guard with him. No sound came from within the barn.

Johnny grew impatient. He couldn't just walk in. Teeter probably had his rifle lined up at the doorway and would shoot at any shadow that loomed up.

But he couldn't stay here all night.

Turning, he eased back and picked up the unconscious guard's rifle. He had to get Teeter out of that barn, and he had to do it fast.

He ran back toward the barn door, keeping close to the wall, and purposely stamped hard across the packed earth. "Teeter!" he whispered in sharp alarm. "The kid's —" He let go with the rifle, levered another shell quickly and slammed another shot into the sky.

For a drawn-out moment no one moved in the barn. Down toward the square men shouted, their voices faint in the distance.

Then someone moved from inside the stables. Boots clunked across the worn boards. Johnny moved quickly. A chunky figure appeared in the doorway, rifle held ready. The man hesitated. "Baker?" he said sharply. "Damn you, if you've let go at a shadow —"

He whirled and fired as Johnny loomed up. He shot from the waist and missed. Johnny's return shot spun him back. He fell inside the barn, and Johnny jumped over his writhing figure. He ran down among the stalls, untied an animal that bulked big in the darkness, and

124

plucked a bridle from its peg on the wall. He wouldn't have time to find a saddle, or get it on his animal.

He led the animal out into the yard, slipped the bridle over its head. The animal was a rangy chestnut. He snorted nervously as Johnny vaulted astride him. "Easy, boy," the orphan said, patting the animal's neck. "We got a long ride ahead of us tonight."

He was out of the yard and across the bridge before the first men came running up from the square. The chestnut swung right along the river trail and, warming up, settled to a hard run.

CHAPTER
FIFTEEN

For a long time Irene Mandell stood rigid against the wall of the booth in the dimly lighted Green Dragon. Johnny Delaney had made his break and gone out the back way, and her father and the others had followed. But the sound of those gun reports remained in her ears, magnified and continuous, long after they faded into the night.

Her body was pressed against the side wall, every line of her rigid and unyielding, as if she would never move again. She was looking down at Iron Mandell. At Henry Mandell, for she had never called him by his nickname, knowing how it rankled in that strange and moody man she had grown up to think of as her brother.

The raw grooves scarring the wood scant inches from her face were reproduced in her mind — for a long time she would remember the wild hate in Henry's eyes.

He lay sprawled on the floor, partially under the booth, a small and pathetic figure curled like some child who had fallen asleep. This was the man even Clay Mandell had feared — a strange combination of ruthless cruelty and almost childish appeal.

Slowly, her legs suddenly weakening, Irene Mandell sank down on her seat and, lifting her hands to her face, began to cry. Silently, unashamedly. The tears ran down her wrists, and she tasted their saltiness.

Clay Mandell came back and found her crying. His long, bony face was stripped of its false piety. He was a hard man who bossed a hard crew, and there wasn't a man riding for him, including Parks, who didn't take his orders. His son, alone, he had not bossed. And though he had often been forced to swallow his anger in front of this boy, he had loved him with a fierce affection he had been unable to convey to Henry.

He looked down on that small, curled body, and slowly the inescapable fact of Henry's death reached through his hard shell to maul him with its bitter truth. His shoulders sagged and he dropped the gun he was carrying. Its thudding made a loud sound in that hushed room, and it roused Irene. She looked up at this man she had called Father, the tears leaving their streaks on her face.

But Clay didn't look at her. He knelt by his son, and in that tragic moment he came as close to God as he would ever get.

The front door opened and a man came running down the aisle, the hard pound of his feet breaking that solemn spell. "Looks like that bobcat got away, Clay," the man said hurriedly. Then, noticing Henry's body, he went silent.

Clay got to his feet. "He won't get far, on foot. Send a couple of the boys in here. And round up Meskill. Tell him I want to see him at my place, right away!"

The man turned and ran out. Mandell looked at the girl then, his face bitter and uncompromising. "I told him to leave you alone," he whispered harshly. "I told him I would handle you. But no — he had to handle it his way. He was going to let this kid cow-poke from up north find you, and then he'd take care of him. But it backfired on him!"

Irene's lips trembled. "My brother — and my father!" She laughed with near hysteria. Suddenly she thought of Johnny and what he must be thinking. Thinking, perhaps, that she had arranged this so that the Mandells could kill him!

"All these years!" she lashed out bitterly, "I've been living with a lie. Hating you, and yet torturing myself, because I thought you were my father —"

"Shut up!" Clay rasped. "With your brother dead you dare say that to me?"

She shook her head. "Not my brother! Never my brother! He told me this afternoon. The real story. My name is not Irene Mandell!"

He slapped her. Almost coldly, his face showing little emotion. It knocked her head back against the boards and brought tears again to her eyes — tears of pain and sudden humiliation.

"You'll be Irene Mandell until the day you die!" he said harshly. "Remember that!"

He turned as two men came toward him. "Pick him up and take him home, boys," he said. He waited until they had picked his son up and left before turning back to Irene.

128

"Henry would have killed me if I had laid a hand to you," he said grimly. "But Henry's dead. He'll never be between us again. I'll have my say with you, Irene, from now on!"

The girl looked at him with a dull, unfeeling hatred.

Irene Mandell sat in the conference room in the rear of the House of Prayer and heard her stepfather repeat his offer of a thousand dollars for Johnny Delaney. Once Clay would have avoided letting her witness these secret powwows, but now he seemed to delight in making her a party to this lawlessness.

One by one she watched Clay delegate men to certain spots in Ladrone, especially the stables where Johnny would probably try to get himself a mount. Finally only Meskill remained, standing uneasily by the wall. The marshal had completely recovered from the muzzle jab in his stomach, but his humiliation would take longer to heal. Nor would he soon forget the riding Clay Mandell had given him in front of the others, when he was still too sick to fight back.

The sky pilot moved restlessly in front of the fireplace. He waited until the others had departed; then he turned and eyed Meskill, as if he had trouble coming to a decision.

Meskill squared his shoulders. "I told you that kid was dynamite!" he defended himself. "Now, mebbe, you'll believe me."

Clay sneered. "It was your job to take care of the tough ones, Skid. That's why we pinned that tin badge on you. Because you talked big about being able to handle anyone drifting through Ladrone!"

"Give me another chance," Meskill muttered. "I underrated him before, but the next time I'll —"

"I'm going to let Parks handle him," Mandell interrupted harshly. "If the boys don't pick him up tonight." He glanced at Irene, sitting stiffly in a chair, her eyes staring at the wall.

"I've got another job for you, Meskill. One you better not fumble."

Meskill frowned.

"I want you to take Irene up to Canyon Verde. Tonight!"

Irene turned her glance to him then, and Mandell's lips pushed out in grotesque smile.

"I'll be riding to Canyon Verde myself in two or three days," he continued. "I want to find her there. You understand that, Skid? I want her there when I arrive!"

Skid wet his lips and glanced at the girl. "Sure," he nodded. "If that's what you want."

"The new herd will be arriving in Canyon Verde in a day or two," Mandell pointed out. "Every man will turn to on the brand changes." He shrugged and turned back to the desk. "The game's up here, Skid. I'm riding down with that herd into Mexico myself this time. And we won't be coming back."

Meskill nodded.

Mandell jerked his thumb toward Irene. "Take her with you, right now. You can make the canyon by morning, if you ride all night." His lips tightened harshly. "I want her out of Ladrone. I don't care what you have to do, Skid — but get her there! Savvy?"

Meskill rubbed the back of his hand slowly across his mouth. "Sure, boss," he said softly.

Twenty minutes later the ex-marshal of Ladrone rode out of town with Irene at his side. They crossed the Mescalero and went past the Toreador, and their passing disturbed the slight man lying with eyes closed on Sally Ryan's bed. Doc Valenti, in one of his rare moments of comparative soberness, was bending over Charlie Payson, while Tando and his sister looked on, and he shook his head, his brow furrowing. "Fifty-fifty chance," he muttered, and then looked up as the riders clattered by outside.

Meskill followed the south trail for several miles before leaving it to strike for the dark hills lifting ragged heads to the sky. Irene followed him silently, knowing the character of this man. A braggart, a man with a wide streak of vanity, a desire to be feared. And like all really small men, unforgiving to whoever cut through the façade he had built up and exposed him for the mediocre hireling he, in fact, was.

Nothing she could say would sway Meskill into disregarding Mandell's strict orders. Nor dared she try to cajole him, for there was a ruthless streak in the man that could easily get out of hand. Only the acceptance of Irene as Mandell's daughter acted as a restraint on this man, for she was alone with him and at his mercy. This knowledge was in Irene as she followed Meskill across the mesquite flats, and her silence was a mask over her numbing fear.

Fear of Mandell's reprisal rode with Skid Meskill that night. But as he put the miles behind him, as the lights of Ladrone grew small and lost in the black night, that fear began to lose its strength. And in proportion resentment gathered power — with each mile he reviewed Mandell's tongue lashing until he fairly writhed in saddle.

Secretly he had always resented the Mandells. He had often fancied himself as the man giving orders. But he had contented himself with the false importance of being marshal of Ladrone, until Johnny Delaney and later Charlie Payson had made him a laughingstock, and Mandell had ridden him with the savage spurs of his contempt.

He was headed for Canyon Verde. Mandell's orders. And all at once he knew he was through taking orders from Clay. It meant passing up his share of the stolen cattle, but the thought scarcely bothered him. He was through taking Clay's order — but more, he was going to hurt that phony sky pilot in such a manner that the wound would never heal.

He turned and looked at Irene and smiled. Iron Mandell had been almost abnormally protective of his sister, and Meskill, not knowing the truth, assumed that Clay Mandell felt the same way concerning his daughter.

Where the earth began to lift toward the ragged hills, Meskill suddenly made his decision. He pulled up and caught Irene's bridle, holding her animal close to his.

He saw fear lick up into the girl's eyes, and he laughed raucously. "What's the matter, Irene?" he leered. "I won't bite you. Not yet."

Her face was white under the stars. "Don't be a fool, Skid," she said, holding back the quiver in her throat. "If my father finds out —"

"He'll never find out!" Meskill sneered. "He'll guess — an' he'll think about it — I hope he does! But he'll never find out — because we're not going to Canyon Verde! We're heading north, right now. A long way north. I've got friends up in the Jackson Hole country."

Hope died almost at once in Irene. Meskill was leaning toward her, reaching for her. He was big and confident and he expected little opposition.

"Might as well get acquainted now," he said. "Don't be a fool, an' you won't get hurt."

Desperation tensed Irene. She felt his hand paw her shoulder, and instinctively she caught at his arm and simultaneously jabbed her spurs into her horse's flanks.

The startled animal jumped forward. Meskill was pulled off balance. His fingers closed on her dress as he tried to support himself. The taffeta tore away in his hand, exposing a white camisole and a smooth, bare shoulder.

He fell awkwardly, while Irene, half sobbing, strove desperately to keep her seat on her frightened mount. His foot slid through his right stirrup and Meskill landed on his back, his head thumping into the soft earth. He swore with sudden fright.

Irene's cayuse made a half-circle as the girl, half out of saddle, yanked thoughtlessly on the reins. The temporarily maddened animal almost collided with Meskill's cayuse. Flying hoofs passed over the dangling figure. Meskill's sudden scream was cut short as a shod hoof thudded suddenly against his head.

Irene Mandell finally got her mount under control. Turning, she saw Meskill's horse plunging across the flats, the limp figure of the marshal dragging from the stirrup.

She caught a half-sobbing breath. The right side of her dress was torn down to her waist. But she was free and unharmed, and relief had its way with her. When she finally sent her mount moving again, she headed north, swinging wide of Ladrone. Ahead of her the Milky Way was like a road of light leading across the velvet sky.

CHAPTER
SIXTEEN

Johnny made a swing into the desert before cutting back south and crossing the Mescalero. He wanted to give the impression to anyone trying to trail him that he was headed back to Mesquite Junction.

A half-dozen miles beyond the creek he stopped to give his rangy animal a blow. The hills hiding Canyon Verde were a vague barrier against the horizon. Johnny restrained his impatience. This was unfamiliar country, and though he had a general idea of direction, he knew he'd have to study Tennyson's map more closely before hoping to find Canyon Verde.

"It'll keep," he muttered as he led the bay down into a coulee and tied him to a mesquite bush. He found a position against the low cutbank whereby he could lean back and stare up at the stars. Without even a blanket to ward off the chill in the night air, this was less than comfortable. But it was safer than a bed in Ladrone.

He rolled himself a smoke and settled back, watching occasional meteors flash across the face of the sky to fiery extinction. He thought of Irene Mandell, wondering if she had been hurt. If she hated him for killing her brother.

Gradually his muscles relaxed and his eyes grew heavy. He flicked his butt away and tilted his hat down over his eyes. He fell asleep.

The bay's snort awakened him. He sat up, and his S & W was in his hand before his mind cleared. The bay had swung around and was looking toward the low hills that loomed up more sharply in the grayness.

With a start Johnny realized it was dawn.

He came to his feet and moved over to the bay, his gaze shifting toward the hills. "What is it, boy?" he whispered.

The bay wasn't jumpy, which could mean that whatever had attracted its attention was not considered dangerous. Johnny climbed up out of the coulee. He kept to his hands and knees, aware that he would present a distinguishable target if he stood up against the lightening horizon.

Two hundred and some odd yards away a horse walked into sight from some dip in the land. A saddled animal. Riderless. Reins dragging. It walked slowly, as if no hurry to get anywhere. Stopping even as Johnny stared to feed at some clump of grass that caught its attention.

Johnny whistled softly. The animal perked up its ears. Johnny eased back into the coulee, wariness tensing him. The animal might have pulled free of its picket rope and just drifted — which meant its rider was afoot somewhere in the vicinity. Or it might be a decoy —

He waited in the coulee while the light strengthened in the east. His bay moved restlessly. The riderless horse drifted slowly, away from the coulee. And Johnny suddenly decided to take a chance.

He untied the bay and mounted. The S & W was in his left hand, held close to his stomach. In this poor light an ambusher would have to be close for a clean shot — close enough for the S & W to hit back.

The big roan shied nervously as he rode up. Its trailing reins snagged around a bush and momentarily checked him. Johnny reached over and caught him by the bit reins. The animal did not fight him.

Johnny shrugged. "Just driftin', eh?" he chuckled. "Wonder who yore rider is — an' what he was doin' out here alone?"

He looked back along the way the roan had come, but the sage flat ran dim and gray under the dawn sky. He slid off the bay, glad to trade that broad, bone-ridged back for the more comfortable feel of a saddle. The roan blew noisily as he gathered up the reins.

"Reckon we'll backtrack a spell," Johnny muttered. He reached for the Winchester that lay snugged in the saddle holster, examined it, and slid it back. He smiled grimly. He was primed for war.

Johnny had not spent much time reading tracks, but he had good eyesight and the trail was plain. He followed the roan's tracks for about two miles, while almost imperceptibly the grayness faded and the sun poked its rim over the eastern hills.

A turkey buzzard floated low overhead, making its first run of the day. Johnny watched it rise in a slow wide circle, and then it dropped. It came down fast, dipping almost to the ground up ahead, lifted upward again and made a quick circle, as if reassuring itself.

Johnny straightened up in his stirrups. "Looks like he's found somethin'," he muttered. He slid the Winchester free and touched heels to the roan. The animal broke into a faster gait.

The buzzard turned to look at Johnny as the orphan rode into view. He had alighted on a man's chest — a man obviously dead — and the carrion-eater was reluctant to give ground before the newcomers.

Johnny's first shot knocked feathers from the bald-headed carrion bird. The buzzard's great wings beat heavily in that morning stillness as it strove to lift itself out of range. Johnny's second shot sent it tumbling to the ground, where its wings beat aimlessly for a few seconds before it died.

Johnny rode forward, sliding the rifle back into its saddle boot. The may lay face upward, and Johnny's gorge momentarily choked him. The entire right side of his head had been bashed in and was almost unrecognizable.

But even without the badge that still glinted from his vest, Johnny recognized the body as Skid Meskill's. He let his gaze move ahead, where a wide trace in the sandy soil was mixed with the tracks of the roam. A trace such as a body would make, if it was dragged head and shoulders downward.

"Slipped, or was thrown, an' his foot caught in the stirrup," Johnny mused. "Horse bolted an' kicked his head in. Finally slipped free here."

138

It was a reasonable explanation, but it did not tell Johnny why the marshal of Ladrone had been riding around the range last night. Nor why a man, presumably born in a saddle, should be unseated by an animal as obviously saddle-broken as this roan.

Curiosity drew him further along the roan's trail. Less than a mile farther on he found a partial explanation. The tracks of another horse joined the roan's, and here Meskill must have fallen, for the wide trace of his body began here.

The other rider, whoever he was, had come with Meskill from Ladrone. From the grouping of tracks here, there must have been an argument. Meskill fell to his death; the other rider swung north, almost directly opposite the original line of travel.

Johnny frowned. He could follow a dozen different lines of conjecture concerning this, but they would get him nowhere. If the marshal of Ladrone had been on his way to Canyon Verde, which seemed likely, his companion had changed his mind.

Johnny considered his course of action. Ladrone was hidden behind him by a rise in the arid land. He had found out all he could in that border town. If Sally Ryan had guessed right, Lew Ferin had been brought to Canyon Verde. Whether or not Lew was still alive was another matter.

It was harder for the orphan to shake Irene Mandell from his thoughts. He'd come back to Ladrone for her, after he had satisfied himself about Lew Ferin. For he had started out to find Lew and now, stubbornly, he knew he had to see it through.

139

He looked down at Meskill and then, overcoming his repugnance, he dismounted and knelt beside the body. The sun was beginning to warm the land as he hoisted the dead man across his saddle and, with the bay trailing, turned his back on Ladrone and headed for the hills.

He rode steadily, pausing occasionally to study Tennyson's crude map. The gambler had put little detail into his drawing, but his landmarks were plain and Johnny easily located them. The sun was riding high in the sky when he came upon an arroyo that gave him his first tangible evidence that he was headed in the right direction.

The arroyo bed, rarely less than a hundred yards wide, was of gravel and sun-baked alkali that resisted the marks of travel. But here and there cattle droppings and the marks of hoofs attested to the use of this dry watercourse as an avenue to Canyon Verde.

Johnny let his gaze run ahead, following that winding watercourse that seemed to run head-on into a spiny ridge of red rock. Heat devils shimmered over the alkali flats and Johnny's eyes slitted against the glare.

That red wall, thought Johnny, would be the barrier enclosing Canyon Verde!

Caution dictated his approach, a caution recently learned. He swung away from the arroyo, heading for a rock-jumbled rise of ground that ran parallel to the dry river bed. Somewhat past noon he had come close enough to that red ridge to call a halt.

140

He secured the roan among the rocks, slid the rifle free, and crawled up that slope until he reached a spot from which he looked down on the arroyo again.

Less than a mile away that dry watercourse snaked through a narrow gap in the barrier enclosing Canyon Verde. Johnny studied that entrance carefully, noting several points along the walls where one man with a rifle could hold that entrance against a posse.

Slowly Johnny let his gaze run with that ridge to the horizon. He shook his head. He doubted if there was another entrance to that hidden canyon within a day's ride.

He shifted his grip on the rifle and was about to edge back when two riders appeared, riding out of the narrow pass. The bigger man turned to wave to someone behind, and Johnny's sharp glance caught the glint of light reflected from a point sixty feet above the entrance. Someone, with a rifle in his hand, had returned the big man's wave.

Johnny smiled grimly. Luck had confirmed his suspicions that the pass was guarded by at least one man.

He waited patiently, while the riders passed within rifle range below. There was something familiar about them both, and suddenly the gloves hanging from the bigger man's saddle jolted Johnny's memory.

Parks and Potsy! The two riders who had followed him and Irene into O'Leary's stable yard. A snarl rose to Johnny's lips, and he had the muzzle of his rifle lined on Parks before he realized that a shot now would kill his chances of entering Canyon Verde.

He held his fire and watched the two riders out of sight. Riding back to Ladrone, Johnny thought grimly: Probably on orders from the Mandells. It occurred to him then that someone before Meskill must have ridden here from Ladrone. And suddenly Johnny grinned.

There was one way to bring that guard down from his perch on the wall flanking the pass. That is, if the marshal of Ladrone had been a frequent visitor to this hidden valley.

Johnny crawled back to where he had left the horses. The roan rolled its eyes at his approach and wrinkled its nose — it did not relish the body draped across the saddle.

The orphan patted the animal's hot flank. "Let's see how smart you are, boy," he muttered. He tied the bay securely, so that the saddleless animal could not follow, and, leading the roan, he left the cover of the rocks. He kept well out of sight of that pass and hit the arroyo where it made a wide bend for the canyon wall.

Johnny's smile was cold. He fastened the roan's reins to the saddle, gave the animal a sharp slap, and stepped back. "Yo're on yore own," he breathed and, turning, headed back for the rocks overlooking the pass.

He crawled into position before the roan came around the bend. Its gait quickened as it recognized the gap in the canyon wall. Johnny shifted his attention to the pass.

Sunlight reflected from a bit of moving metal. Then a man came into sight, crawling down the wall. Johnny could imagine the guard's surprise. He must have seen Meskill's roan often enough to recognize it.

Keeping behind cover, Johnny moved down toward the pass. He was less than fifty yards away when the rifleman appeared, heading down the arroyo to intercept the roan.

Johnny stood up, his rifle sliding up to cover the man. "Hey!" he called. "Drop that rifle!"

The guard stopped as though he had been shot. Then he pivoted sharply and fired in the direction of Johnny's voice.

The orphan's rifle cracked flatly. The guard stumbled, went down to his knees. Johnny swore grimly. He had not counted on the man's foolhardiness, nor the roan's reaction to the shots. For the animal had broken into a run for the pass, and though Johnny made a desperate sprint to head him off, the roan beat him to it.

With the body of Meskill bouncing grotesquely across its saddle, the marshal's cayuse headed through the pass into Canyon Verde!

Johnny stopped and looked back. The run had brought the sweat running down the small of his back. He wiped his eyes with the back of his hand. It would be useless to go back for the bay and try to overtake the roan.

There was only one chance left to him — to follow the frightened animal through the pass. Maybe he could make it through before the appearance of Skid Meskill's cayuse warned the rustlers that something had gone wrong at the entrance to Canyon Verde!

Holding the rifle in his right hand, Johnny broke into a trot down the canyon trail!

CHAPTER
SEVENTEEN

Travelling all night, Bunker had made Canyon Verde by daybreak. He was dog-tired by time he reached the pass and as he rode through he ignored the sentry's greeting. Peeved, the man jeered down at him from his position up on a ledge above the pass.

"Too much town life makin' yuh soft, Bunker?"

Bunker turned in saddle and thumbed his nose up at the man. "Soft," he muttered under his breath. "If you'd driven a wagon across the desert, stopped in Ladrone just long enough for a couple of drinks, got slammed across the head with a gun, an' then had to ride all night to get here, you'd be crawlin' on yore belly, yuh bandy-legged runt!"

Then he grinned, tired as he was, for Bunker was one of those men whose spirits rarely dipped low. He had a sense of humor that kept him on an even keel, even when the going was rough. A chunky man who had started life on an Ohio farm, the youngest of eleven children, he had left home before he was old enough to know right from wrong, and he wasn't even missed.

Now, thirty years later, he had even forgotten his beginnings — nor did he ever question the way he earned his living. In the West of his time, some men worked hard to earn an honest living; others, like Bunker, sought the easier ways of making money. Often they worked hard, but the misconception that dishonesty was more profitable than honesty was hard to dislodge.

The guard's voice had roused him from a semi-sleep, and now his thoughts began shaping what he had to say. Wait until Parks hears about that kid running wild in Ladrone! How he made a monkey out of Meskill! And shaded Pete — and with Pete going for his gun first, too!

Wonder how Parks will take the news? he thought. Parks had discounted Johnny as a threat before leaving for Canyon Verde. Let Meskill chase the kid out of town, Parks had growled.

Bunker grinned to himself. Parks wasn't going to like Mandell's orders. But that was not his, Bunker's, worry.

He turned left as the gap opened to the walled canyon, familiarity blunting Bunker's appreciation of this natural hideout. Locked in by the red-colored cliffs that completely enclosed it, Canyon Verde was a perfect hideaway, fed by springs that transformed the valley into a grassy, tree-shaded paradise in abrupt contrast to the semi-arid and desolate country around it.

Several log shacks and a small corral lay half hidden in a clump of cottonwoods that seemed to grow right under the towering canyon wall. Bunker turned his tired animal down the trampled trail, his spirits lifting as he neared the end of his journey.

A gangling, long-legged boy of sixteen was sitting on a bench outside the cook shack, his left arm bandaged and in a sling. Bunker pulled to a halt in the yard, glanced quickly around and then, catching the boy's half defiant stare, he grinned: "Cook catch you swipin' another hunk of pie, Slim?"

The boy scowled. He had a small, weak-chinned face, full of freckles, and no matter how he tried he never looked tough. "Think I'm a hog like you?" he countered belligerently. He pointed toward the corral. "Broke my arm tryin' to ride Calliope."

Bunker glanced at the horse Slim mentioned — a big white stallion standing docilely enough at the moment in a corner of the corral. "Lucky he didn't break yore fool neck," he grunted. "Where's Vic?"

"Down at the corrals," Slim answered sullenly.

Bunker started to swing away. A short, wiry, leathery-skinned man came to the door of the shack and greeted Bunker. He was wearing a dirty flour sack around his middle, and his jaws worked on a quid, the juice of which stained his stubbled chin.

"Hi, Pip!" Bunker nodded.

Pip wiped the back of his hand across his mouth. "Got coffee on the stove," he invited. "How's things in town?"

"Jumpin'," Bunker answered shortly. "I'll see Vic first. Parks with him?"

Pip nodded. "Potsy, too." And the way he chewed out that statement told Bunker how he felt about that thin, paunchy killer who always rode with Parks. Bunker grinned faintly. "I'll be back for that coffee," he promised. "I'm near dead on my feet."

Slim couldn't pass that one up. "Yo're not on yore feet," he gibed.

Bunker turned to stare at this boy Pip kept around the galley. "Want yore other arm broke, son?"

Slim flushed. "Yuh ain't big enough," he mumbled. But he got to his feet and glanced at Pip, in case Bunker made a move to dismount.

Bunker chuckled as he rode on. He took the path that led through the cottonwoods and came out to the big corrals where cattle stolen from the ranges up north were rebranded before being turned out to feed in the natural enclosure of Canyon Verde.

Three men were standing by the gate, only half watching the activity of the three men inside. There was a fire burning in the enclosure, and a man hunkered over it, holding a straight iron among the brands. Two riders were busy cutting out steers from the bunch crowding the far end of the enclosure, roping them, throwing them and hogtying them. Then the man with the straight iron, a craftsman at brand-blotting, changed the Rocking R to a Circle B.

The three men turned as Bunker rode up. Vic Yaegar, who bossed the crew in Canyon Verde, was a man of thirty — a dark-skinned, taciturn man who rarely got riled. He knew cattle and brands, and he had some education, enough so that the others, out of his hearing, sometimes referred to him as "the perfessor."

Parks and Potsy were with him.

"Thought you an' Pete went to Barasol," Parks questioned him.

Bunker shrugged. "Got back yesterday afternoon. Clay sent me up here. Had to ride all night to make it."

"Tough!" Potsy sneered.

Bunker's lips thinned. Vic he liked. Parks he could take or leave. But Potsy always raised his hackles. The man was like a parasite, feeding on Parks' reputation, drawing his arrogance and tone of authority from the bigger man. Potsy and Parks had been partners before they joined the outfit. They remained close. Where Parks went one always found Potsy. He was, in fact, a mean man, a malicious man — quick to gibe at others, fast to resent a comeback. But bucking Potsy meant having to reckon with Parks, and to date no man had ventured that far.

Bunker held his anger behind his teeth. "You might find it tough, when you get back to Ladrone," Bunker said.

"Who says we're goin' back?" Potsy snapped.

Bunker ignored him and looked at Parks. "There's been trouble," he said flatly. "That kid you ran into at O'Leary's. He's been raisin' the roof. Killed Pete in a shootout at the Casa Diablo — made a monkey out of Meskill. Clay thinks you'd better get back to Ladrone, Parks."

Parks grunted. An ox-like man emotionally, with few ambitions, he yet had a jealous streak in him. "Why don't he get that fire-eatin' son of his to handle the town end? Or is this young tough from up north too much for Iron?"

There was a sneer in Parks' voice, and Bunker caught it, knowing the gun rivalry existing between this big man and young Mandell. On this, however, Bunker was strictly neutral.

"Clay's orders," he answered stiffly. He turned to Vic, standing morosely to one side. "Mandell's gettin' jumpy, Vic. He wants you to get rid of that Rockin' R puncher you been holdin' up here. Dump the body in some ravine where it won't be found."

Vic frowned. "I thought —" He didn't finish what he started, but looked up at Bunker, as if waiting for further explanation.

Bunker shrugged. "Them's my orders." He swung his horse around. "I'm goin' back for coffee an' a bunk, Vic. I'll be stayin' to help you with the brandin'."

He heard Potsy sneer: "Orders! Who the devil does he think he is, Parks? Givin' us orders!"

Resentment burned across Bunker's tanned cheeks. But he was already riding away, and he did not look around, nor wait for Parks' answer.

Pip had poured his coffee into a mug by time Bunker dismounted and stepped into the cook shack. Slim was sitting by the far wall, a Colt held in his lap.

Bunker glanced from the boy to the man washing dishes. For reasons known only to Clay Mandell, this man had been kept captive in Canyon Verde. Usually he was kept tied up in the small stockroom. Evidently Pip had decided to use him in the galley.

"Trouble?" the cook asked. Like Vic, Pip was a taciturn man, with only a meager curiosity.

"Yeah," Bunker answered casually. Now that he had delivered his orders, weariness settled back on him like a load of bricks. He sipped his coffee, found it not too

150

hot, and took a long swallow. It was black and biting and full of grounds, but he didn't complain. Pip didn't take lightly to reflections on either his cooking or his coffee making, and Bunker knew cooks were not easily replaced.

"Meskill can't handle it, so I came up for Parks."

"Good riddance," Pip said thinly.

Bunker got to his feet. He could sense that Ferin was listening by the set of his shoulders. "Guess I'll find an empty bunk an' turn in," he said. "Give me a call for noon chow, eh?"

Pip nodded.

Bunker went out, walked across the small yard to the bunkhouse. He was sitting on a bunk, tugging at his boots, when he heard Parks, Potsy and Vic come into the yard. Potsy was talking: ". . . Take care of Ferin, Vic. I've been waitin' for this since he an' his redheaded partner came to Ladrone . . ."

Vic's sour voice brought a grin to Bunker's lips. "I'll handle Ferin, Potsy!"

Bunker settled back. He didn't want any part of the argument, but he had an idea that even with Parks behind him, Potsy wouldn't win this one. Vic Yaegar was a funny sort of a guy. He could kill in a violent burst of temper, when pushed or goaded. But he hated to see anything get hurt, especially animals . . .

Bunker was still thinking about Vic as he fell asleep.

Slim was kicking his bunk when Bunker awoke. The freckled youngster said laconically: "Chow," and turned away.

Bunker rubbed sleep from his eyes. He pulled on his boots and walked to the door, blinking his eyes at the glare in the yard. Vic was coming up from the corrals. He stopped as he saw Bunker and waited for him. Bunker asked meagerly: "Parks gone?"

Vic nodded. "And Potsy."

They went into the galley together. The other three members of Vic's bunch were already there, sitting at the long plank table. Ferin, under Pip's watchful eye, was serving. Slim was at the far end of the table, holding his own with one arm against the two-handed reach of the others.

Bunker found a place on the bench and looked slyly at Pip. "Mebbe you better shoot Slim an' keep Ferin as yore handy boy," he suggested. "The kid never was much help, even with two good hands."

Slim reddened at the guffaws from the other men. "Aw — shut up!" he said, half crying. He got up and walked out of the shack. The others grinned and went on eating.

Vic ate morosely, as if he had something on his mind. Bunker caught him looking at the Rocking R puncher, and he wondered if that was what was bothering "the perfessor."

They finished eating, and most of the men pulled out Bull Durham sacks and fashioned cigarets. Talk turned to the new bunch of cattle due in any day. Someone observed laughingly: "We got more Rockin' R beef here in Canyon Verde than Rawline has on his range."

Vic pushed his cup away from him with an abrupt gesture. "Ferin!" he snapped. He got to his feet, a lean, wiry, sullen man now, his Colt jutting from his holster, taking on a sudden significance.

Lew Ferin was eating from a tin plate on the stove. He turned at Vic's tone, and Pip moved away from him, reading something in Vic's sultry eyes.

"I've been waiting for you to make a break," Vic said bleakly. "I hate to have to shoot a man who gives me no provocation."

Lew Ferin licked his lips.

"Potsy wanted to do it for me," Yaeger continued. "He has no such compunctions. But I'd sooner let a rattler have you than him."

Ferin said meagerly: "Thanks. So Mandell changed his mind?"

Vic nodded. "Seems we're clearing out of here immediately after the next bunch gets in. Clay only wanted you alive so's he could have a hold over Joe. Long as you were around, and knew —"

The rifle shots trembled faintly in the air, coming from the direction of the pass. Every man except Vic instinctively turned his head toward the sound. One of the men beside Bunker said tensely: "Sounds like Jake's spotted trouble —"

Vic snapped orders: "Pip! You and Slim take care of Ferin. Tie him up and put him in that back room until I get back. Might be just the boys with the herd, letting us know they're coming in."

Bunker was the first to follow him out, the others crowding behind. They crossed the yard to the small corral and saddled hurriedly. Vic moved out first, the others bunching up behind him.

A riderless horse appeared on the trail, heading toward them. A roan carrying someone draped across its saddle!

Bunker pulled up sharply. "Vic — that's Meskill's roan! An' — why, that's Skid across the saddle —"

Vic spurred up and caught the roan's bit reins. There was no mistaking that body. Vic's voice was harsh. "Jenkins, Mike, Poley — let's take a look!"

Bunker hesitated. Then he let the roan move toward the shacks while he swung in behind the others. In a body they swept for the mouth of the pass, and every man had his rifle drawn and ready.

CHAPTER
EIGHTEEN

Johnny reached the end of the narrow pass and cut in sharply for the line of brush growing thick along the towering wall. The roan was already well down a beaten trail leading to buildings half a mile away. The orphan had little time to appreciate the natural beauty of this closed-in valley. He saw men piling out of one of the shacks and later, mounted on horses, come riding up to intercept the roan.

Johnny eased back and waited. They came pounding up the trail in a body. The orphan counted five of them, lead by a dark, close-mouthed man. Of that group he recognized only one — the chunky man named Bunker.

He didn't know how many of the rustlers were here, but he guessed most of them had gone to investigate. In a crouching run, keeping to the cover of the brush, Johnny headed for the shacks under the cottonwoods.

He wouldn't have much time to look for Ferin. Once those men found the guard dead, they would begin a systematic search for his killer. And one man, left in the pass, could prevent anyone from leaving Canyon Verde!

Johnny ran at a steady pace, his rifle held ready across his waist. He slowed down as he neared the shacks and began to move cautiously, thankful for the mesquite that grew up close to the buildings. For as he paused he saw a slim, awkward youngster with his left arm in a sling come to the door of one of the cabins.

Johnny was less than fifty yards away. Slim was staring at the roan with Meskill's body across its saddle. The animal had come to a halt by the small corral, its head drooping.

Slim turned. "Hey, Pip!" he called shrilly. "Meskill's roan just came into the yard, with Skid's body!"

Pip came to the door, muttered a sharp curse, and pushed past Slim. The boy followed hesitantly. The cook reached the roan and lifted up the marshal's head, cursing the flies that swarmed around. Slim gagged and turned away.

Johnny took a chance there were no others around. He broke out of the mesquite, walking quickly, a catlike man with a rifle lined and ready. "Turn around!" he snapped. "An' freeze!"

Slim and the cook did as ordered. Neither man wore a visible weapon, but Johnny took no chances. He scuffed toward them. Any minute now the men who had passed him on the trail would be coming back!

"I'm lookin' for Lew Ferin!" he said grimly. "I'm givin' both of you just ten seconds to tell me where he is."

Slim gulped and edged away, his face turning a sickly yellow. Pip was tougher. He said harshly: "Ferin's dead!"

Johnny's face whitened. This could be the truth. But if it was, someone was going to pay dearly for it.

"Who killed him?" he gritted.

156

Pip's lips tightened. Like Johnny, he knew Vic and the others would soon be back.

Johnny read the stubbornness in this man and swung on the youngster. "*Who killed him, kid?*"

Slim backed away from the look in Johnny's eyes.

"He — he ain't dead —" he gibbered. "He's —"

Pip whirled on him, cuffing him on the side of the face. "Shut up, you fool! Vic an' —"

Johnny stepped in and brought up his rifle butt in a smash at Pip's jaw. The man sagged and fell on his face. Johnny jerked the muzzle to within an inch of Slim's nose, and the youngster went cock-eyed trying to focus on it. He stumbled back.

"Where is he?" Johnny snapped.

"In — in there!" Slim pointed. "In the back room!"

Johnny gave him a shove. "I'm right behind you, kid! Move fast!"

Slim moved fast. They went into the galley, and Slim fumbled at the bolt to the stockroom door. He opened it, and Johnny shoved him inside and followed.

Ferin was sitting on a box facing the door, his hands and feet tied. Johnny stopped and grinned at him, his relief showing all over his face. "Hogtied like a poor yearlin'," he chuckled.

Ferin wagged his head. "I should a known it was you, orphan," he growled. "Only man I know who could cause so much trouble."

"Untie him!" Johnny ordered Slim.

The boy fumbled with the knots binding Ferin. Johnny glanced around the small room with its shelves of canned goods, flour and other staples. It had no window, which made it a good place to keep a prisoner.

Ferin got his hands free and untied his legs, shoving Slim away. "You got here just in time, Johnny," he muttered grimly. "Where's the others?"

"What others?" Johnny growled.

Lew jerked erect, surprise creasing his forehead. "You mean you came here alone? Didn't Red get back to Mesquite Junction?"

"Red got back all right," Johnny nodded. "With a slug through his lungs. He didn't talk much. Died right after I saw him." He gave a brief account of what had happened in Mesquite Junction.

Lew Ferin shook his head in dazed unbelief. "You mean you rode into Ladrone just to show Rawline you could do it?"

Johnny rubbed his knuckles across his bristle. "You want to make something out of it?" he demanded belligerently.

"Yeah!" Lew snapped. "I'm gonna beat some sense into yuh —" He stopped, his eyes narrowing. "Where's Pip?"

"Outside — wishin' he'd kept his mouth shut!" Johnny answered.

"Get him in here," Lew growled. "Vic an' the others will be comin' back in a hurry —"

Johnny was on his way before Lew finished. Pip was on his feet, sagged against the corral bars. He was still dazed, and his broken jaw had swollen so much his face looked lopsided.

Johnny hauled him around and pushed him toward the galley. "You'll feel better out of the sun," he muttered.

Ferin clucked sympathetically at the stumbling cook. "You didn't talk much before," he observed dryly, "but yo're sure as shootin' goin' to talk less for a while now."

He shoved Pip inside the stockroom with Slim and bolted the door. Then he spun around as horses sounded on the trail. He took two quick strides to the window, peered out. "They're comin'," he muttered. "Two of them. Vic — an' Bunker!" He spun around and ran for another door opposite to the stockroom, jerked it open, and disappeared inside. Johnny yelled after him: "Where you goin' — ?"

Ferin appeared a moment later, buckling a worn cartridge belt about his lean waist. "I was here long enough to find my way around," he explained. "That's where Pip bunks. He kept his gun an' belt on a peg by his bed."

Johnny glanced out the window. "Just two of them," he chuckled grimly. "My — won't they be surprised?"

Ferin was checking the loads in the Colt. He stepped up beside Johnny, easing the weapon into its holster, and his voice was suddenly quiet, determined. "This is my show, Johnny. Let me handle this with Vic."

Johnny nodded. "I got a score to settle with Bunker myself," he said, tight-lipped.

Through the window they saw Vic Yaegar and Bunker ride into the small yard and dismount. Bunker glanced at the roan by the corral. Yaegar scowled.

159

"Slim!" he called harshly. "Pip! Come out here!"

Ferin kicked the door open. He stepped outside, with Johnny a pace behind him. Ferin's hands were loose by his sides, a thin smile on his sun-bronzed face.

Vic was like a lean, dour statue, watching him. Bunker had crouched a little, his gaze shunting to Johnny. He licked his lips, remembering how this youngster had killed Pete and humbled Skid Meskill.

"A while back you wanted me to make a break for it, Vic," Ferin said. "I'm takin' that chance now — an even break. But I'm not waitin' until the others come back —"

Vic didn't wait. He went for his gun while Ferin was still talking, and behind him Bunker drew.

Johnny's shot dropped the chunky man before he could clear leather. Ferin's report merged with his, smashing across that sun-beaten yard. Yaegar's teeth showed against his dark face. He took a stumbling step forward, and Ferin's second shot finished him.

Johnny's voice was hard. "Yo're slowin' down, Lew!"

"Let's get out of here," Ferin snapped. "Before the others show up."

They swung into the waiting saddles of the two dead men. "How many left?" Johnny asked as they swung away from the yard.

"Three," Ferin answered. "Poley, Jenkins —" He reined in abruptly. "Look!" Three riders had appeared at the mouth of the pass. They bunched up in a short pause, then came toward them, spreading out fan-shaped as they rode. A rifle made a sharp crack in the afternoon.

160

Johnny was mounted on Bunker's cayuse. He reached for the rifle butt jutting from saddle holster. "Two can play at that game," he muttered. Ferin was doing the same.

The orphan lined his sights on the nearest rider, waited a moment, then squeezed trigger. The man jerked and slid off his running horse, falling limply. That changed the minds of the remaining two. They turned and headed for the pass, and Ferin swore.

"I was afraid of that, orphan! They've got us holed up now!"

Johnny said grimly: We've got to get through, Lew. Maybe if I tried to climb that wall an' —"

But Ferin shook his head. "I think I got a better idea." He swung his horse around. "They'll be waitin' at the other end of the pass, Johnny — waitin' for us to come through. Well, we'll ride through all right!"

Johnny followed him, puzzled but asking no questions. They rode back through the cottonwoods shading the buildings to the big corrals behind where some four hundred cattle were penned.

Johnny grinned suddenly as he got the idea.

Ferin leaned over and unlatched the big corral gate and swung it wide open. Johnny was already riding around the circular enclosure. Ferin waved, and the orphan fired his rifle into the air. He levered another shell into place and fired again.

The cattle milled uncertainly. Ferin joined Johnny, firing his Colt. The stolen beef whirled away from the reports, seeking escape. The ones nearest the open gate ran out. Like a flood breaking through a barrier, the others followed.

Johnny and Ferin came up behind, their shots stampeding the cattle toward the pass. The steers were bunched up close, running wildly, as they poured across the half-mile to the gap that led out of Canyon Verde.

Johnny rode up ahead and turned the lead steers into the pass. He pulled up sharply beside the cliff and waited until the drag went through; then he swung in with Ferin.

The narrow passageway magnified the thunder of those stampeding cattle. Dust rose in a thick, choking pall, obscuring the rear of that drive. Johnny and Lew rode close up with the stragglers, hugging the necks of their animals.

The dust obscured everything. They saw no one, although a rifle cracked once above the din. Then they spilled out to the arroyo beyond. They kept riding, sticking to the rear of that running herd. The stampede began to lose its momentum a mile beyond, and Johnny and Ferin pulled away sharply and drew to a halt.

They looked back, rifles held ready. They saw no one.

Johnny spat out grit from between his teeth. Ferin drew up alongside, wiping his face with his neckerchief. He looked after the Rocking R cattle beginning to disperse across the arid country ahead. He swore grimly.

"It's goin' to take a lot of hard work to round up those cows, Johnny."

The orphan nodded. "That'll be the Rockin' R's worry, Lew. Rawline's job."

"An' mine, kid!" Lew reminded. "I still work for Rawline."

Johnny shrugged. "I didn't come out here because I was worried about Rawline's stolen beef," he said flatly.

Lew put a hand on the orphan's arm. "I'm glad you came, Johnny, even if it was only to show the boys back home that you were man-sized. But Red and I came down to Ladrone to find out who was behind the rustlin'. I found out, Johnny. That's why we've got to get back to Mesquite Junction. I've got a job to finish —"

"Whoa!" Johnny interrupted. "We're headed for Ladrone first."

Ferin scowled. "Why? Ain't you had enough, kid?"

"Not nearly enough," Johnny answered grimly. "I promised a girl I'd help her. A girl named Irene Mandell. Yeah," he said quickly, cutting Lew off before the puncher could protest. "I know she's Clay Mandell's daughter. An' I know the Mandells are the head of this bunch of rustlers. But I promised Irene I'd help her get out of Ladrone."

Lew listened while Johnny recounted all that had happened since he had left Mesquite Junction. The Rocking R man kept shaking his head. "So you got Iron Mandell, too?" he muttered. "Pete, Bunker, Vic —" He tolled them off on his fingers. "Hell, Johnny, there won't be many left for a posse to handle!"

"I'm not waitin' on a posse," Johnny said grimly. "An' yo're forgettin' Parks an' Potsy. Particularly Parks. He's got my brother's gloves!"

Ferin nodded. "I got a score to settle myself, orphan. Back on the Rockin' R. But it can wait. I'll back you in Ladrone, kid!"

CHAPTER
NINETEEN

It was ten o'clock that night when Parks and Potsy rode into Ladrone. They came in across the Mescalero, turned sharply on main Street, and five minutes later they were dismounting in front of the House of Prayer.

Clay Mandell was waiting for them in his back room. He had been waiting since early afternoon, and his impatience was a raw and ugly thing. He had come back to this room after his son's funeral, tired and haggard and wanting to be alone.

Now he got up as Parks and Potsy walked in, and his anger was a strong and violent whip, lashing at them. "I expected you six hours ago, Parks. Didn't Bunker tell you I wanted you here in a hurry?"

Parks scowled. "What's the rush?"

Mandell put his hands on his desk, his fists clenched. "When I send for you, Parks, I want you to come in a hurry. I'm not payin' you to think. Or to ask questions."

Potsy shuffled his feet. "Bunker said some wild kid from up north was givin' you trouble. But we didn't get in a lather over it, Clay. Why, yuh got Skid in town — a half-dozen others, too. And," he added craftily, "there's always yore son, Iron —"

Mandell's face was grim. "Iron's dead. This youngster who signs himself Johnny Delaney on the Come Again register killed him." In clipped, bare sentences he told them what had happened. "That's why I sent Meskill out to Canyon Verde with Irene. The fool should have told you what had happened here —"

"Wait a minnit!" Parks interrupted. "Meskill didn't come to Canyon Verde. Not while we were there, Clay!"

Mandell stiffened. "He left last night. He should have made it about three hours after Bunker —"

"I tell you they didn't get there!" Parks growled. "I don't know where they went — but they didn't go to Canyon Verde!"

Clay Mandell sank back in his chair. Parks' revelation was a shock he couldn't immediately digest. "They left right after Iron was killed," he muttered. "They should have made the canyon by morning. Unless —"

"Unless," Potsy leered, "he got other ideas."

Clay slowly got to his feet. He had waited all day for Parks to show up, and the knowledge that these two men had taken their time from Canyon Verde was suddenly like salt rubbed into the wound of his impatience.

And in Potsy's tone he sensed the disaffection that had always lurked behind the seeming acquiescence of these two men. Coming on the heels of his son's death, Potsy's insinuation was more than he could take.

"Meanin' what?" he rasped dangerously. "What's on yore dirty mind?"

Potsy was standing beside Parks, secure in the bigger man's presence. "Meanin' that yore gal was no angel!" he sneered. "She an' Meskill probably —"

Clay lunged around his desk. "I've taken a lot from you," he said thickly. "But this time you've gone too far!" He got his big, bony hands around Potsy's throat before the other could move. "This time I'm going to choke that insinuating tongue right out —"

Potsy's gun went off abruptly, muffled by the closeness of Mandell's body. Mandell shuddered. Potsy's eyes were beginning to bug in his head. His gun went off again, and again. Mandell arched backward with each report, his long face slackening. His fingers loosened and Potsy shoved him away. Mandell took a step toward his desk, as if looking to it for support. Then, all at once, his legs gave way. He was dead when he hit the floor.

"Damn him!" Potsy gasped. His breath was labored in that still room. The marks of Mandell's fingers were still raw on his throat. He looked quickly at Parks. The bigger man was staring at Mandell's body, his slow mind not yet adjusting itself to the situation.

Potsy wiped his mouth with the back of his hand. The first shock of what he had done was giving way to a strange elation. He had always resented the fact that the Mandells ran the show. It should have been Parks, he thought. He had a doglike devotion to the bigger man who always fought his battles for him.

And now both Mandells were dead!

"He was goin' to kill me," he said thinly. "You saw him, Parks. Just because I said mebbe his gal ran off with Meskill. I had to do it!"

Parks nodded dumbly. "Yeah," he agreed. "He shouldn't have come at you like that."

"Looks like yo're the boss now," Potsy pointed out obsequiously. "I always thought you should be givin' the orders, anyway."

Parks grinned callously. "I was gettin' tired of the whole play, anyway, Potsy. Let's get out of here. My throat's callin' for some of the likker they sell in the Casa Diablo."

Potsy tilted his hat over his eyes. "We'll let the rest of the boys know who's the new boss," he said. "I don't think there'll be any objections."

Most of Ladrone was asleep when Johnny and Lew Ferin rode into town. A small slice of moon, almost lost among the brilliant stars, was poking up over the dark horizon.

Johnny glanced at Lew. "No sense in looking for Irene at this hour," he said tiredly.

Ferin nodded. "You look like you could stand some sleep, Johnny." He reined in and looked down the dark, deserted street. "Got any ideas, kid?"

"I paid for a room at the Come Again," Johnny growled. "But the termites might be watchin' for me to show up there."

Ferin's voice was puzzled. "Termites?"

"Forget it," Johnny said crossly. He glanced back down the street. "We'll try the Toreador," he decided. "I think Tando will put us up for the night." He turned to Lew. "You remember Sally Ryan, don't you?"

Lew nodded. "Tennyson's wife?"

"When did you know Tennyson?" Johnny asked curiously as they swung back across the Mescalero.

"About six years ago," Lew answered shortly. "I was a green kid, working for one of the big outfits around San Antone. Tennyson was dealin' faro in one of the gamblin' houses there." He was silent a moment. "I quit punchin' for twenty a month an' threw in with Tennyson for some big money. We drifted around together for about a year, Johnny." He laughed shortly. "The big money had strings to it. I quit an' drifted this way — an' started workin' for Rawline —"

"That don't sound like an improvement," Johnny growled.

"Oh, Rawline ain't as bad as you think, Johnny," Lew defended the man. "He's been takin' a beatin' this past year. Lost near a thousand head, all told."

They pulled up before the Toreador and Johnny dismounted. The two-story adobe structure was dark. Johnny pounded on the heavy door.

It took some time to rouse Tando. But finally the saloon man's sleep-blurred voice came through the door: "Who ees eet, at thees hour?"

"Johnny Delaney!" the orphan answered.

The door bolts grated softly. The door opened a crack and Tando's suspicious eyes peered into the night. He recognized Johnny, squinted up at Lew still in saddle. His eyes widened. "By all the saints!" he boomed. "Come in! Queek!"

He bolted the door behind them. He was holding a candle for illumination, and the small, wavering flame barely lightened the deep gloom of the room. But Johnny noticed the shotgun beside the door and grinned. Tando was no fool.

"I'll send my man, Carlos, to take care of yore hosses," he said heavily. He walked to the bar and set the candle on it and lumbered behind it like some sleepy bear. "I am steel half asleep," he excused himself. He set out glasses for three and poured tequila in his, glanced at Lew who nodded, and hesitated over Johnny's glass. The orphan made a wry face. "Go ahead," he nodded. "Reckon a jolt of that fire-water is what I need right now."

They had one all around, and Lew joined Tando in a second. The candlelight cast their shadows long and grotesque across the floor.

Tando was chuckling. "Ladrone weel never be the same again, Johnny — after you go —"

"I'm not gone yet," Johnny growled.

Tando wiped his mouth with the back of his hairy hand. "Can I help you?" He looked from Johnny to Lew.

"We could use a bunk," Lew said.

"But for sure," Tando nodded. He held up the bottle of tequila, shrugged disappointedly at Johnny and Ferin's headshakes. "Come," he said, picking up the candle.

They followed the enormous man upstairs. Tando hesitated a moment in the hallway, eyeing the nearest door that was slightly ajar. Johnny crowded up close

170

behind him, sensed Tando's hesitation, and dropped his hand to his gun.

Charlie Payson's voice was a dry chuckle. "Glad to see you again, kid."

Johnny relaxed slightly. "How did you — Hell! I thought you were dead, Charlie!"

"Fooled you," Charlie chuckled. He was standing in the half-shadows, but Johnny could make out that he was wearing a pair of light pants, slippers, and that the upper part of his bare torso was heavily bandaged. Also, he had a gun in his left hand, hanging down by his side.

Tando said, surprised: "You know heem, Charlee?"

"Sure," Charlie laughed. "We met in the Come Again. Johnny didn't like the idea of sharing a room with me."

Johnny turned to Ferin, standing with a frown on his face. "Meet Charlie Payson, Lew — U.S. Marshal," he introduced them. "Charlie — this is the muttonhead I've been lookin' for since I left Mesquite Junction."

Farther down the dark hall a door squeaked. Sally Ryan stepped hesitantly toward them. Her dark hair was loose and long on her shoulders, and a silken wrap covered her night clothes. "Charlee!" she breathed anxiously, and the way she spoke the lawman's name caused Lew and Johnny to glance meaningly at one another.

Charlie reddened. "It's all right, Sally," he reassured her. "They're friends."

Sally came up to stand beside her brother. She looked small beside that massive figure. But the lamplight was easy on her and sleep had softened her eyes. She started Johnny thinking of Irene Mandell, and it stirred a quick restlessness in him.

Lew said: "Hello, Sally."

"I'm happy to see you again," Tennyson's widow said. "Thees ees a surprise —"

Tando interrupted heavily: "I theenk talk weel sound better in the mornin' — si?"

Johnny agreed. "We've had a hard day. But I think I can fill in what O'Leary would have told you, Charlie. In the mornin', eh?"

Charlie nodded. "Sure, kid. In the morning."

The Toreador usually opened at seven, but this morning it remained closed until ten while Charlie, Sally and Tando listened to Johnny's story. Sleep had refreshed the ophan, and he was restless, eager to begin his search for Irene.

Sally had brought breakfast up to Charlie's room. The lawman was propped up in bed, with pillows behind his back. In the daylight his face was a little pinched, pale.

He nodded as Johnny finished. "You've about cleaned things up here," he said. "But it's high time the law took a hand." He turned to Sally. "Where's my shirt? I think I can manage it over these bandages."

Johnny frowned. "Don't be a fool, Charlie —"

The U.S. marshal's voice was crisp, cutting Johnny short. "I'm cutting myself in, kid." He looked at Sally. "If you'll leave us a moment, I'll get dressed."

Sally hesitated. She had lost one man, and she didn't like the thought that she might lose another.

172

"Charlee —" she protested. "The doctor said to keep you off your feet for another week —"

"Doc Valenti isn't a lawman," Charlie interrupted coldly.

Sally looked at Tando, who nodded. Tight-mouthed, she turned and went out.

The marshal swung his legs over the side of the bed. Tando helped him dress. Blood made a dry brown blotch about six inches in diameter on the back of his brush jacket. He tried to lift his arms above shoulder level, but pain brought sweat to his pale face. His mouth tightened with grim stubbornness.

"Reckon I'll have to use a cartridge belt," he said. He looked at Tando. "Do you have a spare?"

Tando said: "*Si* — I get it," and went out.

Charlie looked at Johnny, moving restlessly about the room. "This slug sidetracked me," he said coldly. "If it hadn't been for Sally findin' me and taking me here, Mandell, or some of his crew, would have finished me. I've got a personal stake in this thing, kid."

The orphan turned to face him. "If you think you're up to it, Marshal?"

"I'm up to it!" Charlie snapped. "It's time the law took a hand in Ladrone!" He turned as Tando came in with the cartridge belt. He buckled it on, not showing the effect it cost him. He eased his own Colt into the holster, palmed it, and smiled faintly.

"We'll pick up Clay Mandell first. There's a cell in Skid Meskill's office where we can keep him until I take him back to Houston with me." He looked at Johnny. "Okay?"

"Suits me!" Johnny growled. He had not foreseen this, nor was it to his liking. But Charlie was the law, and had to be obeyed. He looked at Ferin, and the Rocking R puncher smiled faintly and made a gesture with his hands.

They left the Toreador together. Charlie did not feel up to riding, so they walked slowly, crossing the Mescalero and turning up Main. Men watched the trio stroll up the street. But no one tried to bar their progress.

The House of Prayer faced into the square like a beaten dog lying in the hot sun. Johnny put his shoulder to the door and it opened into a large room with benches and a pulpit where Clay Mandell had thundered out against the sins of Ladrone. Johnny's smile was stiff on his face.

They found Clay Mandell huddled on the floor of the back room. He had been dead for hours. His body was cold and stiff when Johnny turned him over.

Charlie said wearily: "Looks like someone beat us to him."

"Parks an' Potsy got in last night," Johnny said grimly. "Could be they had a fallin' out with Mandell —" The implications of this sickened him. He had expected to find out the whereabouts of Irene from her father. With Clay dead, he might never see Irene again. Unless Parks knew!

He swung on his heel.

Charlie said: "Where you going?"

"To find Parks!" Johnny growled. He shouldered the lawman aside. Charlie winced. He made a grab for Johnny as the orphan strode out. "Hang it, kid —"

He stumbled and nearly fell. Ferin caught him and helped him to a chair. "You better rest awhile, Charlie," he said. "No use overdoin' it."

"Johnny —"

"Can take care of himself," Ferin finished smoothly. "You take it easy for a few minutes. I'll be back —"

The marshal pushed him away. "The devil you will!" He got to his feet. "The law's been ignored entirely too much in this town. I'm coming with you!"

Johnny found Parks at the Casa Diablo. He knew the big man was in there because there was a horse tied to the rack with Johnny's boxing gloves hanging from the saddle. He didn't hesitate. He shouldered through the batwings without looking back — not seeing Ferin and Charlie Payson cut across the street behind him.

Parks was at the bar, talking to one of the percentage girls whose painted face and dull eyes still showed the effects of sleep.

Johnny glanced about that gambling hall. There were not more than a half-dozen others, most of them grouped around a card table. Potsy was nowhere in sight, and Johnny forgot him as he turned his attention to the big man who had manhandled him back in O'Leary's stable yard.

Parks heard his step, glanced in the mirror behind the bar, and whirled, his hand slapping for his Colt. The girl stiffened against the counter.

Johnny's Smith & Wesson stopped Parks. It was levelled at the big man's stomach, and there was death in Johnny's eyes, cold and uncompromising.

"Where's Irene Mandell?" he asked tightly.

Parks shook his head, his hand falling away from his gun. "I'm not her keeper," he said warily, trying to read what was behind the youngster's question.

Johnny thumbed the hammer back on his S & W and Parks' shoulders hunched forward. His face paled. "Darn it, kid," he said quickly, "she left Ladrone last night with Meskill. Headed for Canyon Verde. That's what Clay Mandell said before —"

"Before you killed him?" Johnny snapped.

Parks' gaze shuttled to the rear door, and mentally he cursed Potsy. "I didn't kill Mandell," he denied harshly. "Potsy said somethin' Clay didn't like an' he tried to choke Potsy. Potsy shot him. But I don't know any more about his daughter than I just told you!"

Johnny was thinking back to the tracks he had followed in the country south of Ladrone. It must have been Irene who had been with Meskill. After the phony lawman's death she had headed north. Relief eased the dry tightness in his throat. Maybe he'd never see Irene again, but at least she was free.

Unconsciously he found himself knuckling the bristle roughening his jaw, and his grin was sudden and hard, matching the temper in his eyes.

"You had this comin' since that day in O'Leary's," he muttered. "Unbuckle yore gun belt!"

Parks glanced toward that rear door again. *What the devil was Potsy waiting for?*

He unbuckled his belt and let it drop to the floor. At Johnny's command he kicked it away from him.

Johnny holstered his gun and slowly unbuckled his belt. He rolled it around his weapon, his smile twisting to a sneer. "O'Leary said you had the biggest mouth in Ladrone," he said bleakly. "I'm gonna make a few changes around it, right now."

He placed his belt on an empty table and turned toward the man backed against the bar. Potsy came out of the rear door then. He came out with a gun in his hand, his narrow face screwed around his gloating smile. He couldn't resist taunting Johnny as the orphan stepped in mid-stride, turning to meet Potsy's harsh laugh, and that moment cost him his life.

A gun smashed flatly from the batwings. The heavy slug slammed Potsy back against the framing as he was squeezing his trigger, and his bullet went wide, smashing among the bottles behind the bar. His body twisted slowly, trying to bring up his gun again, and at the second report from the batwings he went limp, crumpling to the floor.

Charlie Payson pushed through the batwings, followed by Lew Ferin. Charlie's gun was still smoking.

Johnny turned to Parks, who had not moved from the bar. "Yore hole card wasn't good enough," he sneered.

Parks lunged at him. Johnny sidestepped and cuffed him across the head, and as the big man whirled, he stepped in and sank his left hand wrist deep in Parks' middle. That punch hurt the big man; he never fully recovered.

The Casa Diablo had seen many fights within its confines, some of them more vicious. But none had been more brutal than the beating Parks took at the educated hands of this smaller man from the ranges across the desert.

Parks was big and tough. But he didn't have the stamina of his lighter opponent. And time and again Johnny sank his fists into Parks' midsection, until Parks was floundering around, wheezing, his ribs and stomach raw and aching, his face a bloody pulp.

A man ran into the Casa during the fight with the news that a posse was coming up the street. But he went silent as Ferin menaced him with his gun. Slowly he backed against the wall, and watched that grim fight raging in the middle of the big room.

Johnny finally finished it. A left hand spilled Parks across a table. It collapsed under him, and he lay beaten and still among the wreckage.

Johnny let his hands fall by his sides, his chest heaving as he dragged in air. His shirt hung in shreds from his muscled shoulders. His face was bruised; one eye had a rapidly growing mouse over it. Blood trickled in a red thread from his mouth corner.

He found his belt and buckled it around his waist. Charlie Payson was smiling, a new respect in his eyes. "I never saw a man take a worse beating, kid."

Johnny pushed past him to the street. He was through in Ladrone. Rounding up Rocking R beef, and cleaning up at Canyon Verde, would be the Rocking R's job.

He paused on the walk, squinting. The square seemed full of riders. Someone yelled: "Men — there's the orphan!"

178

He ran his gaze over those bunched men, picking out Sheriff Marasek, Macey Rawline, Joe Arlen, his uncle Andy. And — Irene Mandell!

She was sliding down from saddle, a small, dusty, begrimed figure, but with a gladness in her eyes that brought Johnny's shoulders back and put a smile on his bruised lips. She ran to him, and he put out his arm and held her. And in that moment Irene Mandell, herself an orphan, knew she was no longer alone.

Behind Johnny, Charlie pushed through the batwings. He stopped to face the bewildered posse, his smile thin. "Reckon you came just a little late, Sheriff. The shindig's over!"

"He shore has!" Ferin added grimly. The Rocking R man stepped out from behind the marshal, his gaze settling on the Rocking R foreman sitting saddle beside Macey Rawline.

Joe Arlen stiffened as he saw Ferin.

"Yeah, I'm alive, Macey," Lew said harshly. "Thanks to the kid here. An' I found out what Red an' I came to Ladrone for." He paused, smiling bleakly at the look on Arlen's face.

"I found out who was behind the Mandells, boss. I found out who made it easy for these rustlers to raid Rockin' R an' Sleepy H beef." He took a step toward the unsmiling ramrod of the Rocking R. "Tell, Arlen!" he snapped harshly. "Tell them how you've been robbin' Macey Rawline for more than a year — playin' a doublecrossin' game on the man who fed you —"

Arlen made a break for his gun. Ferin's hand went up and his gun smashed Arlen off his horse.

"I owed Red that," Lew muttered.

Marasek shook his head. "Looks like we came on a long, hot ride for nothin'," he said, smiling. "The party's sure over."

"All except one thing," Johnny said grimly. He looked at Rawline, sitting stunned in saddle, and slowly ran his knuckles across his beard-roughened jaw. "Have I grown that beard, Macey?"

Macey grinned weakly. "You shore have," he conceded.

Marasek was smiling. Irene was standing beside the battered orphan, and Marasek was thinking that maybe this girl would do what no man in the Big Bow country could — tame the kid!

He sure hoped so — for the future peace of Mesquite Junction.